12·13·12

For Patricia

Warmest regards

Walter Thompson

SHADES OF ORANGE WITH MANY GREENS

SHADES *of* ORANGE *with* MANY GREENS

Visions of Paul Cézanne

a novel by

WALTER E. THOMPSON

LANGDON STREET PRESS

Langdon Street Press
212 3rd Avenue North, Suite 290
Minneapolis, MN 55401
612.455.2293
www.langdonstreetpress.com

ISBN-13: 978-1-936782-80-2
LCCN: 2012932035

Distributed by Itasca Books

Paul Cézanne (French, 1839-1906)
Mont Sainte Victoire Seen from the Bibémus Quarry, c. 1897
Oil on canvas
25 1/8 X 31 1/2 in. (63.8 X 80 cm)
The Baltimore Museum of Art: The Cone Collection, formed by Dr. Claribel
Cone and Miss Etta Cone of Baltimore, Maryland, BMA 1950.196
Photography By: Mitro Hood

THE FLOWERS OF EVIL by Charles Baudelaire, Translated by James
McGowan (1998, OWC): First 24 lines from "A Carcass" (pp. 59-61) & first
two lines from "Correspondences" (p.19) By Permission of Oxford University
Press

Author photo attribution: Photo taken by Antony Gravett
Cover Design and Typeset by Madge Duffy

Printed in the United States of America

For JOYCE,
who never let me quit, both times

CONTENTS

ACKNOWLEDGMENTS   *ix*

TO THE READER   *xi*

1   STILL LIFE WITH BASKET OF APPLES   *1*

2   THE CAFÉ   *25*

3   THE FIRST VISITATION   *35*

4   MONT SAINTE-VICTOIRE FROM THE QUARRY   *57*

5   GIVERNY   *71*

6   CEZANNE'S DREAM   *86*

7   THE SECOND VISITATION   *98*

8   A LONG DAY IN AIX   *124*

9   BRIEF BUT FIRM   *164*

10 LUNCHEON ON THE ROCKS   *165*

11 RUE LAFFITTE   *178*

12 THE THIRD VISITATION   *197*

13 HOUSE BELOW A RIDGE (A PAINTING IN PROGRESS)   *212*

AFTERWORD: WITNESS   *214*

ACKNOWLEDGMENTS

Much thanks is owed to all those who encouraged me to redo this book, which was published originally as *Another Cézanne*. The new title, *Shades of Orange with Many Greens*, is more focused, as the text now offers a more refined expression of the artist's visual process and adds elements that expand the portrayal of his character. I owe many of the changes and revisions in this edition to my wife Joyce, my son Paul, and my copyeditor Scott Stackpole.

Scott came on at first to help me with very basic copy matters, but almost from the beginning, he went much deeper into the work, discussing with me many aspects of consistency, character, word flow (and word choice), and logic of ideas. He was most patient and generous with his time, reading and rereading my efforts and helping make them clear and dynamic. He served me very well as a sounding board, for which I will always be grateful.

My wife and son have seen me through both editions of this work and have delivered some tough love, not holding back when I made a wrong turn or a bad choice. Joyce, especially, has never wavered in supporting me in this rather quixotic endeavor to render a meaningful picture of Cézanne through devices of fiction.

Since this new edition retains a great deal of the content from the previous work, I must mention the names of at least five persons whose timely help greatly aided me at various moments and places in the evolution of that first edition: Anne McKay, Tim Yohn (sadly deceased), Sal Federico, and Jim and Ann McGowan. As before, I have included excerpts from Jim's excellent translation of Charles Baudelaire's *The Flowers of Evil*, which was published by Oxford University Press.

I have held back, until here, the name of Joel Isaacson (Professor of Art History, retired, University of Michigan), who read and encouraged me in the first edition and who has been very supportive in this second endeavor. Thank you, Joel. And finally a latecomer to help me has been Steve Kogan, whose timely entrance into the process greatly enhanced the afterword, "Witness."

Finally, I owe my deeply felt thanks to the folks at Langdon Street Press, who have helped me so much to bring this work to fruition for a second time. They have been prompt, courteous, and smart at every moment I needed them. I especially thank Laine Morreau, my editor at Langdon Street Press, for his superb work on my manuscript.

TO THE READER

Some words of explanation are owed to you, dear reader, before you turn to the pages of *Shades of Orange with Many Greens: Visions of Paul Cézanne*. In an altered form, this work was published fourteen years ago in England and distributed in Great Britain under the title *Another Cézanne*. This new edition, published here, seeks a readership in America.

With the exception of "Afterword: Witness," which did not appear in the original version, what I have changed is more related to language than content. The concepts, ideas, and structure of the earlier work are largely preserved in this new edition. Certain uses and refinements of language are meant to make the ideas clearer and more precise than before.

Paul Cézanne is hailed in our time as one of the greatest painters of the modern era. Largely forgotten today is that for most of his lifetime he was subjected to decades of abuse, neglect, and scorn by most of his own generation. Cézanne was more than fifty years old before the first significant signs of recognition appeared, and this work is concerned with the period before he began to gain that success.

This narrative attempts to broach three themes. The first theme questions how the man just described could work for decades in the face of virtual failure and rejection. The second theme touches on the complex state of the painter's own personality, one in which doubt, fear, and mistrust plagued him at nearly every turn. The third theme concerns his artistic practice, especially the unique manner in which he looked at the world he painted.

My own career as an art historian and a painter come together here, permitting me to form the story I tell, a story that represents five years of writing and research but many more years than that of steeping myself in his art..

The mode of accomplishing these ends has led to an unorthodox arrangement of events. The book, strictly speaking, is neither biography nor art history but instead draws freely and deeply from both of these literary forms at the expense of chronology.

Since the issue is not the order of things but the essence of them, I have arbitrarily chosen what, in my judgment, are the best and most revealing works and events, regardless of their historical place in time. The works chosen and the events cited have been picked solely for their efficacy in recreating the man and his work.

Getting as close as possible to Paul Cézanne has always been a recurring dream of mine. To meet and be in his presence in some way has been a continuing desire for many years. In that time I have had numerous encounters and conversations with him in my imagination. In its own way, this book is my endeavor to bring forth the most fruitful and interesting of those conversations and encounters. What I am unable to do in a literal way, I've tried to achieve through a literary form. Therefore, you deserve to know from the start that, while every chapter is an invention, it is informed by what is historically known and by what is there to be seen in the paintings. Trying to pull apart the fact from the fiction would be like trying to separate the food from the seasonings meant to enrich and enhance it.

Besides the artist himself, the chief figures in the narrative who are historically real are Claude Monet, Pierre Renoir, Camille Pissarro, Philippe Solari, Émile Zola, and Ambroise Vollard. The chief characters who are fictional are André, Maurice, Roger, Alain, Nicole, and the stranger. Other personages mentioned—such as other artists, critics, and writers—all refer to historical figures. Only the depiction of the director of the museum in Aix (Chapter 8) is pure fiction, symbolizing and reflecting my own disgust at how Cézanne was ignored and so badly treated by the "cultured" art world of Paris and by the residents of his own hometown.

> W.T.
> Taghkanic, NY
> 2012

1

STILL LIFE WITH BASKET OF APPLES

PAUL CÉZANNE ROSE FROM HIS CHAIR CURSING, "Damn it, why won't it come?" The old painter struck the table in front of him with his fist, rattling the crockery and sending the apples tipping and rolling. He watched one apple drop to the floor and roll slowly past a small cabinet crowded with paints and brushes. It came to rest halfway inside the perimeter of a dark shadow cast by a tall, freestanding cupboard. He idly noted the fullness and clarity of that part of the apple's contour that caught the light flowing in through the studio windows; the apple's opposite edge, more difficult to see, lay buried in shadow.

Having no interest whatever in retrieving the truant piece of fruit, the old man turned back to the objects before him. In spite of their insensate nature, they seemed to return his gaze in dumb and scornful defiance. No matter how hard he stared at them, they seemed to willfully withhold the promise of even a modicum of cooperation in his difficult endeavor.

His frustration mounting, the painter rose from his chair a second time and surveyed with distaste the apples, dishes, and bottles in front of him. They made no sense. For some time now, he had been struggling to compose these intractable things into a workable still life, but he was now on the verge of giving up altogether and starting over.

He looked down without enthusiasm at his handiwork. Standing motionless, he drew his right hand over his full white moustache, then slowly stroked his goatee. Leaning over, he moved one of the apples to the left, nearly closing up the space between it and a shallow porcelain bowl. This small change was a half-hearted attempt to heighten the tension between the apple and the bowl by narrowing the distance between the two, but it was hopeless. He was forcing things, and he knew it. The arrangement still lacked a unifying idea, and this playing with details was useless.

The end came soon enough. He reached across the table with his right hand and took up one of the vessels standing among those he was contemplating. With his left hand he pushed aside the rest of the objects into a meaningless pile, a state of affairs he instantly ignored.

Actually, it was not a table at which he was seated but a few boards set across two wooden boxes. The real tables here in his studio were already encumbered with other still-life arrangements, one that he would almost certainly abandon and two others for which he still held out modest hope.

The single object he had rescued from his sudden dismantling of the still life was a small ceramic jar, cylindrical in shape and tan in color. He sat down again to study this piece of crockery. The only interruption in its straight sides was the shallow groove that encircled its body a half-inch below the rim. The part above this groove was glazed dark brown, forming a substantial decorative band around the top of the jar. The opening of the little vessel was covered by a flat lid, glazed in the same dark color as the band. He removed this cover and set it aside.

Holding the piece down toward his lap, he looked intently at its curving exterior as he gently rolled the round form from one hand to the other. The light coming into the studio through the tall north windows caused a bright highlight to form playfully on the convex surface. This thin white emanation, as if trapped inside the transparent glaze, swam and wiggled up and down as he gently turned the little vessel back and forth.

Were he to paint the jar at that moment, he sensed a subtle presence of what he would translate into blue and green tonalities arising to alter the warmth of the tan-colored clay. Holding the jar there between his legs, this tendency toward blueness increased due to the piece absorbing light from his trousers. Raising the jar up again above his lap, a warmer spectrum of color—as if drawn from the surrounding air—reasserted itself. Where the curving surface went up against his hand, the color changed decidedly over to the red and yellow range, the shiny glaze absorbing and reflecting the warm pigmentation of his own tanned skin. Reflected light was an ever-present influence, always working to alter local color.

Cézanne turned the piece upright and looked inside at the circular bottom of the jar. In the glazed surface, he saw floating there a dark, broken, barely recognizable image of his own face. It came and went depending on the angle at which he tipped the piece. In the slow movement of his hands, an ever-shifting play of shadows, highlights, and colors rolled, climbed, and bounced off the interior walls of the container. With each tilt of the little pot, the circular opening assumed a different elliptical form and rearranged the interior shadows and reflections, creating with even the tiniest movement a slightly altered composition. In the conventional sense, the small container was empty. But to Cézanne, the jar's interior was filled with a complex array of optical events that he watched and studied intently.

He held the jar at arm's length for a moment, feeling its weight and memorizing its shape. Then he set it down in isolation on the side of the table away from the chaotic pile of rejected objects. Something was wanted to go with this piece that was not to be found among those objects just disposed of. Half turning in his chair, Cézanne's eyes roamed around the studio searching out other objects scattered here and there in the large space.

The pieces he had collected over the years were ordinary enough: various plates, assorted jars and bottles, a few vases, a short-stemmed drinking glass, a fruit bowl. They were common pieces of ceramic, porcelain, and glass with little or no intrinsic value. He had culled most of them from among the discarded or rarely used crockery and glassware he found in his family's attic and pantry. The two pitchers, the teapot, and the sugar bowl had floral motifs painted on them, but mainly he was drawn to those vessels that had strong shapes and one or two clear colors.

Several of these had been around him for years, appearing over and over again in his paintings, especially the blue ginger jar, the dark red rum bottle entwined now with faded wicker wrappings, the green and white olive jar, and the fat-bellied jug. Then his eyes came upon the plaster cast of the little winged figure, a copy in the round of a Baroque putto. He had from time to time used this smiling child in his paintings too, but it would not do now.

Another set of objects that had appeared recently in Cézanne's work, darker and more somber than any so far mentioned, were several human skulls. Three of these grimacing forms were now carefully placed on a table, across which lay a richly patterned rug with folds carefully bunched. This was one of the active still-life groups on which he planned to continue working.

It had long since ceased to be a matter of setting a few things down on a table in order to paint them. Over the course of years, the selection and placement of these still-life objects had taken on an immense importance. Once arranged, the grouping became the subject of long and intense study, often occupying Cézanne for months. So right there from the start, the form, color, and exact location of every object mattered a great deal. He had to consider the interval between each thing chosen, and the angle of the light falling upon it required the greatest attention. In recent years, creating one of his still-life arrangements had become a kind of meditation all its own, long before pencil or brush were taken to hand.

Now the old painter rose from his chair and crossed the studio to an open shelf where he stored a number of his precious objects. He chose a long-necked wine bottle, whose tall tapered shape and deep, dark color attracted him. This elongated form made a strong contrast with the squat jar he had already set aside. He then selected a pale gray mustard pot, slightly taller and fatter than the jar. This piece, like the other, had straight sides, except toward the top where they curved gracefully into a flat rim edged by a heavy lip. As he came back to his workplace with these new finds, Cézanne spied a large wicker basket with a pair of curving handles, which he placed on the table with the other two objects.

He went about clearing the work surface of the clutter created when he pushed aside his failed project. He quickly took everything off the table except the two ceramic jars, the wine bottle, and the basket. The apples, however, he retained, putting half of them in the basket, nearly filling it.

So here was a new start.

Once seated, he began moving the jar, the wine bottle, and

the mustard pot into various groupings, one in front of the others. He placed an apple in front of the jar. From the particular angle of his vision at that moment, the apple's red skin crossed in front of the right side of the little ceramic vessel, forcing a new visual configuration that included both objects. From this line of sight the jar could no longer be contemplated in its fullness but had to include the apple. Partway down the straight side of the jar, its edge burst out into the curve of the apple's contour. This was the stuff of straightforward vision, undiluted by the habitual mental adjustments that always separate objects from one another in the mind's eye. From a purely optical point of view, the apple and the three overlapping containers were one visual entity and that fusion, in turn, a part of the larger setting that surrounded it.

What Cézanne still lacked, however, was what he called a motif. This is what he had been seeking without success all morning: some felt quality or relationship that came from the objects themselves that would guide him in his effort to organize and give meaning to the things he grouped together.

The painting of still life was a major activity for him, equal in interest to any other subject matter. Years ago, these modest bits of glass, crockery, and pieces of fruit—so perfectly suited to his slow and deliberate methods of study—seemed like stepping stones to more complex and ephemeral configurations in nature. In the beginning, Cézanne thought he had only to master their simple shapes and colors in order to pass into more difficult forms. But when he began working on these compositions, the problems that emerged as he tried to see and paint them gradually took on far greater complexity than he could at first imagine. The effects of light and color on space and form, coupled with the impact of his own visual process, grew increasingly challenging. In the end, his still-life studies formed the principal gateway by which he entered into serious investigations of nature and perception. Now, more than three decades later and after thousands of hours of patient labor in front of his beloved objects, they were still the chief means by which he studied the physical world.

In order to approach this new study in a different way, Cézanne decided to incorporate a piece of drapery. In his previous attempt that morning he had worked with his objects on the hard, bare surface of his makeshift table. The careful manipulations of the folds of the drapery would give him many new opportunities to bring together or separate his apples and containers. From among a selection of fabrics he had collected for this purpose, he chose a simple white tablecloth set all around its borders with a thin, pale red band.

The artist again cleared the space before him. He spread out the cloth, pushing it around until it was centered. Then he turned the whole on an angle, forming a diamond shape. Next he pulled the cloth forward until the nearest point of the diamond fell well over the front edge of the table. Then he folded the right-hand corner of the drapery over itself. This created a triangular shape, white on white, on top of the remaining cloth. Now he had a new field onto which to set his objects.

This time he placed the basket of apples in the left rear corner of the table. Because of the basket's size, he sensed immediately that the whole arrangement would have an emphasis in that direction. In an instinctive acknowledgement of that situation, he gathered some of the material of the tablecloth into a long diagonal fold, lining it up at the front of the table and angling it directly back to the basket of apples. He even fluffed up a part of the cloth, letting it overlap in front of the basket. Now the diagonal axis across the table was not merely implied; it was visibly expressed by the strong movement of the folded table-cloth. Then the painter propped up the basket, tilting it forward so as to make the contents more visible from his angle of view.

None of these choices so far constituted what Cézanne would consider his motif. They were simply tentative ways of manipulating his objects and activating the space around them. It was a matter of getting a feel of things while he searched for the meaningful pattern or idea. The still life, properly named, would not begin to appear until this organizing principle emerged. Until then, he had before him merely a random group of unrelated objects.

He paused to consider where to locate the tan jar and the mustard pot. After a couple of unsatisfactory tries, he simply set them together in the middle of the table, the jar overlapping the pot. In the same state of uncertainty, he put the wine bottle near the basket and then turned his attention to the distribution of some of the individual apples left over after he had filled the basket.

The fruit had been left by his gardener, Vallier, who regularly supplied him. This particular morning, Cézanne found a box filled with a variety of apples of different colors—red-, green-, and yellow-skinned. He placed a half dozen of them on the white cloth, moving them in various positions and combinations without achieving an arrangement that satisfied him. Doubt plagued him at almost every step in his work, even here in this earliest moment of his process.

He added more apples, considered their placement for a few moments, then took some away. It was such a simple problem and yet so capricious and elusive. Whatever arrangement of apples, none was better than any other. He could do anything. Without some defining or overriding idea, nothing much mattered. Time passed, and he grew restless. The same problem he had faced in the earlier effort still confronted him: the motif that would give order and purpose to his arrangement would not come.

Now the urge to stand up and walk around overcame Cézanne, a sign that things were not going well. He slowly paced around the studio muttering to himself, a curse or two audibly passing his lips. He gazed at his objects from the other side of the room, as if the distance between them and himself would somehow enable him to see the whole more clearly. He walked back to the table where, without sitting down, he pushed the wine bottle up against the edge of the fruit basket, merging these two forms. Then he reestablished the mustard pot and the tan jar, which had been situated near the middle of the table, back on a line parallel with the bottle and the basket. This opened up the whole front half of the tabletop for a freer play of the apples.

He stood there looking intently at this new disposition of things. However deliberate and thoughtful the whole process seemed, it was driven by pure intuition. He could not predict or rationalize a solution ahead of time; there was, in fact, no *one* solution. His efforts were directed to a moment when the forms before him would coalesce under the force of some governing idea into a configuration that stirred him. Until he achieved this moment of conviction, he had no meaningful choice.

Cézanne started pacing slowly again. He glanced up distractedly and saw himself in the big mirror in the far corner of the studio. This unexpected sight of his own face broke his concentration. He crossed the room and stood pondering his own reflection as if it showed him an image of someone he could barely recognize. An unkempt, grizzled-looking figure stared back at him. He had been and still was in one of his periods of extreme isolation, shunning nearly every human contact. Besides his wife and his son when they were in Aix, only his sister and his gardener were allowed access, and these two persons rarely intruded on his solitude, never staying long or trying to engage him in frivolous talk.

Cézanne stood staring at himself, his eyes wandering over the bulges and depressions of his aging face. He noticed the tightening of the skin crossing his cheekbones; he saw the redder, looser flesh filling the hollows beneath his eyes and the skein of wrinkles that turned in and out of his facial structure in nearly perfect cadence. He studied the shadows in the sunken spaces to either side of his nose where it joined his brow, defining the complex planes of his eye sockets. He looked carefully at the upper and lower eyelids, which in their curve and thickness formed the elliptical openings through which his eyes peered. He was at this moment half the observing artist critically investigating the aging process he saw and half the acutely feeling human being reacting emotionally to the implications of that aging.

He leaned closer to the mirror and looked directly into his own eyes. He could see his dilating pupils quiver, the tiny blood vessels marking up the dull whites of his eyes. He blinked several times, shook his head hard and, in a scoffing tone—the human being in protest—said angrily, "What does it matter?"

But as if it did matter and the ruminations were not yet meant to have an end, he saw to his right another presence gazing with vacant stare back at him from out of the reflections in the mirror. A few inches away and at the same level as his own face, the reflection of a fourth skull stared dully at him. It lay on a shelf behind him in a cupboard across the room. The sudden image of the two heads, side by side but in such different states, startled him.

He passed his gaze over the swelling contour of the skull's forehead, while with the forefinger of his right hand he traced the same curve of the bone pressing against the skin of his own head. Looking at the reflection of the empty eye sockets, he felt the bone under the soft skin of his own cheek just below the eye. The skull revealed the construction upon which the form of his own flesh depended.

The skull also proclaimed something else entirely. Though mute and expressionless, the skull, in terms that could not be plainer, bore vivid witness to the old artist's mortality.

Shaking himself, Cézanne tried to throw off this sudden dark mood. He looked away from the foreboding skull and concentrated on his own reflection again. Gradually his mental focus was superseded by the visual habits of years. The artist in him took over.

He began noticing the patterns of light and shadow across his own face. By slight movements of his head up and down or right and left, he could adjust and readjust the distribution and emphasis of forms: now his brow and nose were highlighted, now his left cheek. Each movement resulted in a new and different arrangement of light and shadow. Then he began viewing his upper body in the context of what surrounded it there in the mirror. He studied his head and shoulders protruding into the studio space behind him. The rectangular mirror framed everything like a painting, the distant cupboard containing the skull standing along one of its edges.

He moved his head and shoulders ever so slightly. Held in one place, the reflection of his head touched the reflection of the skull there on the surface of the mirror. But if he moved his head slightly higher, the two were no longer on the same horizontal plane. He bent back a little farther, again shifting the location of the skull relative to his own face. That piece of bone thirty feet away in the studio was here in the mirror right beside his face. That was how it was in painting; real depth collapsed and everything ended up on the surface of the canvas. The near and far brought together, sometimes even touching, even though in reality the two things might be far apart. The mirror here, like the canvas, was the great leveler. Real depth was altered by its transference to the flat plane.

This image of himself in the mirror reminded Cézanne of his unfinished portrait of Geffroy, an exhausting undertaking with more than eighty sittings in Geffroy's large apartment in Neuilly, a district on the western edge of Paris. Some of the problems then were similar to those he had just contemplated in the mirror: how precisely to place the head and torso in its context and how exactly to bring them together with the setting.

In the painting of Geffroy it was a matter of the elaborate fireplace and the tall bookcase behind the sitter who posed seated at the desk in his study. Cézanne finally found the answer only when he put the corner of a book, which was on the bookshelf several feet behind Geffroy, up by his sitter's right cheek. This created the accent he needed there and, more importantly, was the pivotal element that let him anchor the figure to the background.

Cézanne remembered now with a smile—though his mood then was far from jovial—how Geffroy had pleaded with him to continue working on the painting. He had gone far with it, but in the end he could not go on. Geffroy was unable to understand what it cost him in energy and effort at the late stages of his paintings, when it was a matter of trying to bring together into a seamless whole all the complexities of his vision. He finally gave it up. Still, he had made some good progress, he thought.

Cézanne turned and looked across the studio at the scattered apples and displaced containers. It was time to have another try at getting the apples to work and the other objects to somehow comply. He slowly crossed the large room and, settling into his chair, aroused once again his powers of concentration.

He sat for a long time looking at the objects in front of him. He moved various things around, mainly the pieces of fruit, always searching for a seminal idea. As time passed, he found himself looking more and more closely at the way the two groups of fruit were constituted—some packed tightly within the circular confines of the basket, others freely scattered across the loose and pliant folds of the drapery. The rigid sides of the woven container forced its pieces of fruit into a compressed mass that contrasted sharply with the flat and open surface where the remaining apples were strewn. The different character of the two types of boundaries intrigued him—the one firm and intractable, the other entirely open across the plane of the table's surface.

Cézanne began spreading out the loose apples even further throughout the fabric, half hiding some and completely exposing others among the white hills and gullies of his terrain of drapery. He varied the spacing among them, letting some stand alone while grouping others together.

As the idea took hold, he placed a half dozen other apples just beyond the border of the cloth, on the bare table itself. This seemed to stress all the more the difference between the closed confinement of the one bunch of fruit and the loosely dispersed arrangement of the remainder. These two very different arenas of containment were coming together now in his mind, suggesting to him that they could be the organizing idea he had been searching for all along; this could be his much sought-after motif! The longer he studied this arrangement, the clearer it became and the more excited he got.

Cézanne smiled as the idea grew in his mind. He continued experimenting with the placement of various apples among the folds, gradually elongating the group of them so that they contrasted as vividly as possible with the tightly packed mass in the basket. He molded the fabric around and between the apples, trying to give each piece its own individually shaped backdrop of space.

In the course of more play, he gradually formed a shallow arc of apples across the top edge of the cloth. This led to a decision to reinforce the curving line of fruit by reshaping the top edge of the tablecloth into a loosely formed arc of its own. His composition was turning into a complex play of curves of various sizes. The arc of the cloth and the curve of the basket were like powerful statements of a theme, under which the small, tight curves of the fruit were playful subthemes. Curve blended into curve as Cézanne carefully adjusted each apple in relation to ones next to it. And as counterpoint to these curvilinear movements, he molded the drapery around the fruit into contrasting straight and angled forms.

Now a wave of fatigue came over him, and he felt sudden pangs of hunger. He had been working for a long time. He should have stopped earlier to eat something. Not to do so risked fatigue or, worse, dizziness and even nausea. With mild diabetes, he had to be careful, though that did not mean that he always was.

He crossed the room in search of the bread and sausage he had brought with him that morning. Arranging a chair near the still life so that he could put his feet up on a box, the painter laid out a small meal on his lap and meditated on the morning's work. Back in his chair he tried to eat something, but he was too preoccupied to sit for more than a moment. He perused the arrangement, looking closely again at the pattern and distribution of the apples.

Suddenly he realized that for some time, he had paid little attention to the wine bottle and even less to the ceramic jars. He studied the configuration made by the basket of fruit and the wine bottle beside it. The tipped position of the basket seemed to call for a corresponding gesture from the bottle. Putting the food aside, he went up to the table and carefully placed a couple of coins under the bottle to make it lean very delicately toward the basket. This action satisfied him as far as it went. The bottle and the basket were pulled more closely together, and the tilt of the bottle reinforced the diagonal movement of the drapery from the front to back of the table.

He was up again, talking to himself as he paced the studio. He stood across the large room looking from afar with a disgruntled stare at his objects, especially the small ceramic jar and the mustard pot. He did not like them anymore; they were not right for the still life as it was now evolving. He went on walking until he noticed a shallow plate lying on a table among the objects of the still life he had already scavenged. Its white porcelain surface gleamed in the bright light. He picked it up and slowly went back to his makeshift table.

Cézanne stood for a while before his new project, ruminating with the dish in his hands. Finally he leaned forward and, with one hand, removed the mustard pot and the jar, putting them to the side. With the other hand, he set the porcelain dish in the place where they had stood. As he made this exchange, he knew instantly that he had done the right thing. Both the color and the shape of the plate reinforced important qualities elsewhere in the grouping: the whiteness responded to the cloth and the roundness reflected the shape of most of the other objects.

Cézanne studied this new addition and decided it needed to be raised slightly higher in order to be more effective. He went to a bookshelf in his studio and selected a thin volume, which he carefully placed under the plate. But now this flat, empty surface required something in it to mute its visual force. Left as it was, its severe geometry and gleaming whiteness gave it undue prominence. The piling up of more apples was an easy choice, though he refrained for the moment from such an obvious solution. It struck him that the introduction of a different kind of object in this place might be a welcome change.

Again Cézanne went around his studio in search of something that would serve his purpose. As he rummaged through a cupboard, his hand found a crumpled paper bag filled with something soft and squeezable. When he opened the bag he found a dozen or more ladyfinger cookies. At first he could not think how they had gotten there, having no memory of ever bringing them into his studio. His gardener, who posed for him two days prior, must have left them.

The instant he saw these pale yellow forms, he knew he had what he was searching for. He had used ladyfingers in another still-life painting years before. He emptied the contents of the bag onto the white plate and moved the cookies around into different piles. There were ten pieces in all. As he had done in the previous painting, Cézanne stacked the long rounded pieces in twos, each pair turned in the opposite direction from the pair below. This made an orderly stack five layers high, and he eased himself back into his chair to study his handiwork.

The whole thing was starting to work now. There was something about the built-up structure of the stack of cookies that represented a third kind of distribution of elements. Some things were confined by the strict limits of the container that held them, others were strewn openly across the cloth and table, and these last things delicately rose in a structure created out of their own self-sufficiency.

The empty wine bottle, like a surrogate observer of all that surrounded it, teetered in the middle of all these events like some bemused bystander, its tilted axis, however, abetting the thrust of the composition to the left. Its strong vertical presence commanded a central position among the three arrangements of objects. The bottle functioned as a kind of hub around which the three groupings were displayed.

Finally Cézanne had achieved his goal! This brought to a close the first phase of his new still-life project, at least for the time being. The objects appeared well enough integrated into a unifying idea; their exact placements, however, would still be subject to scrutiny and adjustment as the painting process went forward. The basic color relationships also were in place, though these too would undergo subtle alterations as Cézanne worked with paint and brush.

It was never simply a matter of bringing the still life to this point, then merely copying it onto his canvas. It was never a matter of copying it at all. In the selection and arrangement of the objects, Cézanne had gone as far as he could go. His motif defined, the transfer now of the three-dimensional objects to the two-dimensional plane of the canvas would move the work to a sphere where other issues could be addressed. He would experience and analyze the array of sensations that his own arrangement of reality evoked.

It was time to prepare his paints and set up his canvas. He employed a large range of colors, which he laid out on his palette in a logical order: first the yellows followed by the reds, then the greens and blues. The number of different pigments within each set of hues allowed him a choice of several tints in each color group with a minimum of mixing. Holding his palette on his lap, he sat back in his chair for one last survey of all his preparations.

When he was finally satisfied, he put his palette down and reached for some brushes stored in a jar located on a small wooden stand to his right. He inspected their condition for a moment and then lightly worked the bristles of two of them at once into the palm of his left hand. As he did so, he looked up again at his still life, now with fresh curiosity.

He was in a changed frame of mind. The ritual of laying out the colors signaled the start of a new, deeper, and also more perilous stage of his artistic process. Here was another opportunity to begin again, to launch one more assault on what more and more seemed to him the impossible task: the expression of the full range of the sensations he felt before nature. The seriousness with which he approached these endeavors was what made them so excruciating. His self-worth as a person and as an artist was at stake. A new painting for Cézanne was an event that carried within it both hope and risk in generous parts.

He arranged around himself the tools and materials of his art, including various oils and solvents, and set a canvas in place on the easel. Then he fell again to scrutinizing the still life he had so patiently created.

Over the years, his manner of looking had become a subject of the keenest interest to him. He gradually realized that he could not stand apart from the world he perceived with complete impartiality because whatever he saw was unavoidably filtered through his own mental and perceptual apparatus and subject, therefore, to the nature of that operation. Everything he looked at—the objects in a still life or the rocks and trees in a landscape—formed a situation in which he, as observer, played far more than a neutral or disinterested part. Whether by intention or accident, his processes of apprehension influenced the things he saw. Of the myriad things present at every moment in one's visual field, he, as viewer, made a choice or was attracted to some relatively small and specific place in the field. His seeing started there and moved outward according to the needs or predilections of his will. In effect, he saw what he chose to see.

Especially in the still lifes, over which he spent long weeks and months, Cézanne cultivated habits of looking that substantially departed from the rapid, more fluent ways that one normally views the world. With utmost deliberateness he slowly and patiently studied his objects in all their many parts, searching out, as much as he could, every nuance of form and color, edge and surface. He often looked for long periods of time at a single contour, trying to sense its weight and value in the context of what surrounded it. The clarity of an edge was very susceptible to change, depending on what it was seen against.

Within the constraints of this special practice, he became aware in new ways of his own visual focus. When he concentrated on the edge of one form—a contour of one of the apples before him, for example—the apple behind it was not as visually crisp and clear until he moved his eyes to it. In which case, the edge he was just looking at blurred a little bit. There was a minute discontinuity between points of focus.

In normal seeing, of course, the mind instantaneously compensates for this, and what we experience is a seamless clarity. But in the course of years of this special looking, Cézanne had rediscovered this primitive awareness, and its implications for him were stupendous. He found that he actually perceived objects in the world by a process that took place in infinitely small gradations of time. To him, seeing the world all at once or in a single, unified glance was an illusion. Visual comprehension of even the smallest or closest objects occurred in minute steps in time.

Thinking about this in a slightly different way, each place where his eyes paused became a zone with its own center in the midst of a larger, less distinct peripheral field of forms. Each tiny movement of his eyes to another place resulted in a reorganization of that visual field and a change to another zone with a different focus and an altered periphery. In the course of normal everyday looking at something, we sweep across the field of viewing and all the indistinct changes are received and discarded with such deftness that our consciousness barely, if at all, notices them. But Cézanne's procedure of looking, brought to such extreme and thorough slowness, made the presence of these peripheral conditions unavoidable.

When slowed down this way, Cézanne's perceptual process became a continual pulling into focus of a tiny segment out of his general visual field and then letting it go again as another segment was momentarily pulled into view. To see one side of a thing with perfect clarity meant surrendering a clear view of the other side; both, even up close, could never be seen with the same clarity at the same instant. This was true whether looking closely at objects in a still life or from afar at trees and hills in a landscape.

In a way, seeing was about presence and absence; the tiny part just seen forever retreating into the larger, blurred horizon as the next tiny part came into focus. The whole of anything seen this way was a compilation of this succession of the ever-focusing and refocusing eye. Eventually this mode of seeing began to creep into Cézanne's art: the visual field not as a seamless whole but as a dynamic field of linked parts, even down to the movement of the eye across the skin of an apple.

Cézanne had come to understand that seeing, in its most basic and primitive state, was not a passive or disinterested viewing of the world; it was a complex and active exchange in which, by the consent and power of his will, he went forth and seized the things he saw from out of the endless flux and flow of horizons that perpetually surrounded him. To imbue his paintings with this dynamic process gradually became deeply important to him.

The profound difficulty and irony here was that this level of visual experience was buried so deeply in the subconscious of human beings that rarely, if ever, did it get noticed. People were as little aware of this subtle process as they were of breathing. It meant nothing to them in their daily intercourse with the world, however much they used it all the time. Yet here he was now trying to arouse a consciousness of this process and incorporate it into his art for others to see. The burden of his painting lay somehow in finding a way to suspend the conventional habits of seeing in order to allow people to see anew. Thus, he forced upon the objects he painted these effects of his own visual process, which led, in the most extreme cases, to distortions for which he paid a high price because in the beginning these displacements and exaggerations were so misunderstood.

Cézanne thought of the time he had tried to explain some of this to his old friend Philippe Solari, but it was plain very quickly that Philippe did not understand. It was not much different with Pissarro or Monet; he could not get them to sustain enough interest in these ideas either. At certain moments like this, the frustrations due to his lack of success raised doubts about his methods, and this brought on almost unendurable depressions.

Cézanne had trained himself to be sensitive to this level of perception at great cost to himself in time and energy.

As his mood grew blacker, he looked harder at the apples before him. He snatched one of them up in one hand and held it very close to his face. With a smile tinged with bitterness, he remembered the vow he had once made to paint an apple that would stupefy the Paris art world. He had dreamed that by means of an object as ordinary as an apple he could reveal the complexity and mystery of the visual world that existed everywhere. In a single apple he wanted to make these Parisian fools see what goes on around them even in the most trivial and commonplace circumstances. Right in front of them! Right under their noses!

A moment passed, and the old artist shrugged as he returned the apple to its place in his still life. Then he reached for a pencil.

He rarely made separate, preliminary drawings or other studies of a subject he was about to paint. Instead he went directly to his canvas, setting down there the few lines he needed to guide him into the work. He aimed for the most generalized and least encumbering visual skeleton around which he could then build his brushstrokes of colored pigment. In his view and in his practice, it was during the very act of painting that drawing was accomplished. For him, drawing and painting were utterly intertwined.

The placement of each stroke of paint not only expressed the light and color values of the object but at the same moment contributed to its form. Both the drawing and the painting were complete when they reached together what he called their "plenitude."

Cézanne's mode of painting belonged to a tradition that went back at least to the Venetian Renaissance, where the visible brushstroke was maintained as an active part of the finished work. In the hands of many great artists of the past—Titian, Tintoretto, Rembrandt, Velazquez, Watteau, Delacroix, and Courbet among them—the brushstroke served many descriptive as well as expressive functions. Manet and the Impressionists were part of that tradition, and so was Cézanne.

The brushstroke set up a parallel reality within the image. It preserved a physical manifestation of the pigment and a visible embodiment of the artist's presence, almost like a fingerprint yet so much more. The vigor or the energy or the delicacy of the stroke could express great feeling and reveal what Cézanne liked to think of as the "temperament" of the painter. The constructive nature of this kind of painting—a slow and deliberate filling up and filling out by one brushstroke after the other—suited his temperament perfectly and gave it free rein.

His sketch drawn directly onto the canvas was hardly more than a rough map, a kind of spare and broken geography that designated the general location of his still-life objects within his composition. No single form was enclosed entirely by the light, loose lines. The shapes of individual apples were suggested by broken arcs, the contours of the wine bottle were discontinuous segments, and the basket and cloth were equally open. His intention in such a drawing was to establish the placement of things while maintaining as much openness and freedom of choice as possible.

As Cézanne examined his sketch, identifying the points most crucial to the structure of the forms before him, the white of the canvas flowed through everything and lay waiting for the first strokes of colored pigment. When applied, these would begin shaping and separating one segment of space from the next. Each mark of the brush, with its own individual shape and tone, became a unit in the whole that had to be locked together with others around it, the aggregate of brushstrokes forming a kind of interconnected tissue. Cézanne knew from long experience that making those linkages of color to color, stroke to stroke, could cost him dearly. There were many times when he was unable to complete these passages across a form.

But now the moment had come. Cézanne took up a brush and separated out on his palette some cobalt blue, which he lightened slightly with white, adding sufficient medium until the paint was thin and semitransparent. The brush held before him, he fixed with his eyes the edge of one of the apples in the still life and then found its corresponding place on the canvas, laying down as he did so two strokes of thin, watery color, one to either side of the broken outline in the drawing before him. These thin blue marks immediately evoked a feeling of air and space. The very shape of each stroke of pigment, by the way it related to the other, created a sense of form springing to life.

Now the painting was engaged, and the cunning old artist rose to the challenge. Before his eyes, the forms and colors bounced and cavorted in a free and irrepressible dance, daring the painter to arrest and discipline them.

2

THE CAFÉ

IT WAS LATE AUGUST IN PARIS in a year made memorable
by the successive number of days in which the thermometer rose
above 95 degrees. On this particular day—unhappily no different from those preceding it—the heat caused the air to shimmer
and the relentless brightness of the sun to blind anyone fool-
ish or careless enough to look into it. At the hottest part of the
day, those who could took refuge in the Café des Arts on the
Boulevard de Clichy, seeking what little relief there was available in the airless shadows of the interior. Even the waiters, their
white-sleeved arms folded idly across black vests or hanging
limply against immaculate aprons, stood stoically at their sta-
tions, as if by their stillness they could stave off the worst effects
of the heat.

This torpid scene was altered suddenly by the commotion
of three young men, who in defiance of all reasonable behavior
brusquely entered out of the blazing heat and sunshine, their
laughter and loud talking bursting like a small explosion upon the
quiet that hung over the muggy interior of the café. The waiter
nearest the door looked at the barman, who rolled his eyes and
shrugged. At the sight and sound of this miniature invasion, the

heads of customers turned listlessly to observe the trio pass in single-file along the narrow space between the closely packed tables.

"Oh, how can they?" was the universal but unspoken sigh.

As oblivious to the heat as to the clientele, the young men settled themselves around a small table in the alcove at the rear of the café. They immediately ordered glasses of beer from the waiter who had followed them down the aisle.

Maurice stroked his scruffy beard as he scrutinized his two friends. "Didn't I tell you? You've never seen better painting!"

He was referring to three works by Paul Cézanne they had just seen in a paint dealer's shop around the corner on Rue Clauzel.

Maurice's height was matched by his girth, and his indifference to his grooming was a continuous source of amusement to his companions. His dress gave him the slovenly look of someone stuffed into ill-fitting clothes. His mind and tongue, on the other hand, were as clear and sharp as his appearance was careless and rumpled. Although he was an aspiring young sculptor, he was, above all other living artists, passionate about Cézanne the painter. Argumentative and intense in his ardor for Cézanne's painting, he studied his two companions closely for the least sign of reluctance to agree with him.

André sensed immediately Maurice's readiness to pounce at a wrong or hesitant word and neatly avoided the bait with an offhand remark. "For a while there, I thought Tanguy was not going to let us see his Cézannes. Did you notice how he seemed to put us off, Roger?"

André's verbal sidestep did not faze the always overly serious Maurice, who continued his stern surveillance of his two companions.

"Yes, I noticed Tanguy's reluctance too," replied Roger. "He's so protective of his Cézannes, you just never know which way he'll turn. I think your remark about having overheard Gauguin praising Cézanne's painting changed his mood."

André, half-smiling, turned back to his earnest friend and chided him. "Relax, Maurice, you won't get us to bite. We love him too, you know. Go find some of his detractors and tell them they've 'never seen better painting.' Go tell that to Rochefort; I'd love to see that. He hates Cézanne."

André spoke these words in good humor. He knew how much Maurice always spoiled for an argument.

"That ass? What does he know?" blurted Maurice. "He even hates Zola! Did you read that ridiculous article he wrote the other day about both of them?"

"Yes, I read it. What did he call it? 'A cult of ugliness.' He accuses them both of ugliness."

André's appearance could hardly have contrasted more with Maurice's. Medium height, slight of build, and well groomed, he was the only son of a prosperous Parisian businessman who doted on him, indulging the young man's half-formed ambitions to be a writer.

André's attraction to a circle of young artist friends had brought him into contact with the most recent art, especially the Impressionists. Through constant exhortations by Maurice and others, he had become passionate about the paintings of Cézanne, even though the works he had seen firsthand were not many. It could be said in truth that few people, even close friends, had seen many of the painter's works in recent years.

André laughed as he nudged Roger, who spoke up as if he had not heard the exchange between the two friends. "Did you see Tanguy hovering around us? He was listening to every word we said."

Roger, the youngest of the three, was a student who had become attached to one of the academic studios to which young painters apprenticed themselves. He had considered, then rejected, entering the Beaux Arts Academy, whose reputation had steadily declined. Lately he had even become disillusioned with the course of his private studies, partly due to Maurice's persistent ridiculing. As Maurice had done to André, he drew Roger to the work of Cézanne and his circle. Roger now embraced the new art that was still viewed by many as radical even though it had been visible to the public for more than twenty years. Roger now felt a passion toward this art that was the equal of his friends.

Unlike dark-haired Maurice and André, Roger was blond, clean-shaven, and prematurely balding. He was thin and wiry with very fair skin. Some part of his clothing almost always bore evidence of his artistic pursuits; flecks of paint could usually be seen on his trousers or his coat, and a smudge of dark red paint now marked one of his sleeves.

"Yes. Thank God for Tanguy," said Maurice as he gestured to the waiter for three more glasses of beer. "Cézanne's paintings are rejected without fail at the Salon, and even the private dealers won't touch him yet—the fools. So poor old Tanguy is all we have for now."

The waiter brought the drinks, and as he turned to leave, Roger rose to his feet, extended his glass, and in a voice loud enough to turn heads at nearby tables, made a toast: "To Cézanne! May he triumph tomorrow over the imbeciles who deny him today!"

André and Maurice raised their glasses in approval of Roger's toast, and all three took swallows of beer.

"My God, those apples!" said André. "That little canvas consists of just seven apples. Nothing more. Aren't you glad you're a sculptor, Maurice? Think of competing with that! When Roger here paints, he must try to rival him."

"Except in Cézanne the painters today have a leader; they have a direction," replied Maurice. "If that were the case for sculpture too, I would welcome the challenge."

As they sat down again, Maurice continued speaking. "Yes, those apples positively pulsate, not only with life but with subversion. It's as if he wants to reinvent the apple—not for eating, mind you, but exclusively for looking at. His apples are objects to be ingested by the eye alone and digested in the mind. They are things to be studied. There's more visual truth and excitement in one of his apples than a whole sky full of Bouguereau's cherubs."

Bouguereau was a frequent target for these young men, especially because of his outspoken hostility to Cézanne and his Impressionist friends, and this scornful barb thrown at one of the most prominent Salon artists made all three of them laugh again.

André, his eyes bright with mischief, flicked the sleeve of his large friend.

"No, Maurice, you miss the point. There's eating intended in those apples. At the sight of them, Cézanne would like old Bouguereau to eat his words. He'd like those apples to stick in his throat."

More laughter erupted between André and Maurice as they turned toward Roger. Their friend had become detached somewhat from their mirth as he pursued a different line of thought. Suddenly he erupted excitedly in a different vein. "What about the other still life with the flowered drapery? There's a kind of tumult in those folds, as if they were waves. The ginger jar, the sugar bowl, and the plate, all cocked at different angles, bobbing up and down in that turbulent sea of folds."

He stared into space as if still seeing the painting in his mind's eye. "All those colors in the porcelain," he went on. "It seems every color is there, and still they all come together as white! How does he do it?"

"You're the painter," teased Maurice. "You tell us."

"Émile told me that Cézanne spoke to him of wanting to paint black and white by using all the colors of the spectrum," said André.

"Ah, that extraordinary friend of yours, Émile Bernard," said Maurice, with a touch of sarcasm in his voice. "Bernard spent a month with Cézanne in Aix, didn't he? He went right up to his door, unannounced and unknown, and was welcomed right in. What astounding luck! Cézanne is famous for avoiding just about anyone who comes up to him unexpectedly, even his friends. This friend of yours must have the hypnotic skills of a magician."

André laughed. He knew Maurice was more or less correct in what he said, but it was the envious way he said it that was amusing. The thought of Bernard having such friendly and pro-longed access to the painter made Maurice almost crazy with envy. Maurice loved to speak about a conversation he would like to have with Cézanne, but this had always been in the realm of fantasy until he found out that Émile Bernard had done just that.

"I suppose he even watched Cézanne paint," said Maurice.

"Ah, there you go too far," replied André. "You know as well as I, no one watches the old man paint. Not even his best friends. On the rare occasions when he goes painting with Renoir or Monet, for example, even they must let him set up in a place where they cannot see his brush touching the canvas."

André paused, expecting Maurice to jump in with some angry or sarcastic comment. When Maurice remained silent, André continued his description of Cézanne's peculiar habits.

"And when he does portraits, even his sitters hardly look at him. They sit as still as stones and as silently too. They know that the slightest movement or sound might upset him enough that he will suddenly stop working, pack up his things, and leave. He treats his sitters as if they are still-life objects. It's remarkable!"

"Yes," added Roger, "and speaking of his still lifes, I've heard he paints for so long on them that sometimes the flowers wilt and the fruit rots!"

"Émile told me something even more incredible," continued André, pursuing this topic of the old artist's oddities. "When Émile was in Aix with him, Frenhofer's name came up."

"Balzac's Frenhofer?" asked André.

"Yes, exactly. Balzac's fictional character. Cézanne blanched at the mere mention of his name! Can you imagine? Émile couldn't believe his eyes or ears. Cézanne is haunted by Frenhofer. He identifies himself utterly with Frenhofer's dilemma as a painter. Émile said Cézanne got up from his chair, his features contorted, and pointed repeatedly at himself, as if he were Frenhofer! At first Émile could not calm Cézanne down..."

Hearing this, Maurice could no longer contain himself and exploded angrily. "That's ridiculous! Frenhofer was insane. He committed suicide because he could not paint. That has nothing to do with Cézanne. Not only can Cézanne paint, he's the sanest, most cerebral painter I know."

"Of course," said André, "but you must admit these eccentric..."

Maurice cut him off. "Who's to deny it? Cézanne is a very odd fellow. He's totally unpredictable. Irrational, even. So what?

Next, I suppose, you'll tell me how he often throws his work away in a rage, that people find his paintings hanging in trees on hillsides around Aix. Or in his garden; I've heard that one too. And that he can't stand to have people touch him. And that he actually thinks Gauguin is trying to steal his sensations. And that he hides himself as if he fears life itself, avoiding even people who love him best. I know all that; and to all that I say, 'So what?'"

The sternness in Maurice's voice seemed to impose a silence on his friends. He went on speaking with only slightly diminished intensity. "All these eccentricities pale beside the one task he has devoted his whole life to. He paints like no man living or dead, and who cares about these quirks and contradictions? Not me!"

Pausing, Maurice took another swallow of beer and continued speaking, though now in a calmer tone. "The poor devil needs as many of us as are willing to speak up for him, you know. He's been vilified and slandered more than any of the others. The art mobs never stop harassing him. But in spite of it all, he keeps working all alone down there in the South. And think about this: if you don't happen to know about Tanguy's shop, where would you ever see a Cézanne? He's never had a show, he has no art dealer…just a painting or two in group shows long ago plus these few paintings over the years at Tanguy's. It seems like his reputation has been built mostly out of rumors and far-fetched speculations. It's crazy. At the same time, he's both known and not known. It's really very peculiar."

Maurice's long speech on behalf of his hero trailed off in quiet rumination. His verbal effort seemed to take him through the gamut of emotions, from anger down to quiet contemplation and sadness. André and Roger sat quietly, somewhat awed by

Maurice's intensity and sincerity.

Before any of the three spoke again, they heard a familiar voice call out André's name. Looking up, they saw a young man coming toward them who all three knew very well. Rising from their chairs, they greeted Alain who, like Roger, was a young painter. "Well, look at you," said André. "You look very excited. What's going on?"

"What's going on?" repeated Alain. "I just ran into Le Bail, who told me that Cézanne is going to have a show here in Paris!"

All three burst forth at once, their questions rapidly following one upon the other.

"What show?"

"Where?"

"What are you talking about?"

This news was astounding, hardly to be grasped in the first minutes of hearing it. Finally, after so many years of neglect, Cézanne was going to exhibit his paintings. All three friends assailed poor Alain at once.

"Who's giving him a show?"

"A solo show?"

"When?"

"How did this get arranged?"

"Where will it be?"

"Who talked Cézanne into…?"

Alain laughed and reached out with both hands to calm his friends. "Sit down. Sit down. One question at a time. I'll tell you everything I know, which at this point is not much. Le Bail got the news from Émile Bernard, who heard it, I think, from Pissarro. I guess Cézanne agreed to the whole thing just a few days ago. He's going to have a show at that new little gallery on

Rue Laffitte. You know the one. The dealer's name is Ambroise Vollard."

"It sounds impossible," said Maurice. "As far as I know he's never had a one-man show anywhere. Why now suddenly?"

"Yes, I know," said Alain. "But whatever the reason—and who cares!—it's evidently going to happen at last. Monsieur Vollard has somehow persuaded him to show a large group of his paintings. Think of it. It will be magnificent! Le Bail didn't know if the exact date has been set yet. Probably sometime in November or December. Before the end of the year, at any rate."

"How ironic," said André. "It's taken a young upstart dealer to dare to make happen what for so long has seemed it would never happen. I wonder if Vollard knows what he might be in for?"

"Don't worry about that," said Maurice. "I commend him for his courage, whether it's founded on innocence or shrewdness. Whatever brought him to this decision and however he managed to bring it to fruition, I congratulate him. Think of it. We will finally get to see a large body of his paintings all at once!

As if it had been rehearsed, everyone rose to their feet and cheered at once. The sudden burst of sound shocked everyone else in the café, all of whom turned, aghast, toward the cheering young men.

"Oh, my God," said the waiter to the barman, "how can they?"

3

THE FIRST VISITATION

WITH STRETCHED CANVAS and folding easel strapped to his back and paints and brushes in a pouch at his side, Cézanne slowly climbed the steep and rocky slope to the place the local inhabitants called "the caves." They were not caves really but a precarious piling up of boulders that, by some magical juggling act of nature, managed to cling to the slope of the steep hill above the Château Noir. The larger crevices between the rocks inspired the name. It was just these rocks and the growth around them that had recently attracted the painter's interest.

Trees and brush found precipitous footholds, and other, smaller forms of vegetation filled the narrow fissures and little ledges, making a rich contrast to the massive larger stones. The old artist was particularly drawn to the acute angles at which the ground rose and the rocks tipped. Even the trees grew aslant.

He was here in countryside he had known all his life. This was the very place he had wandered as a boy with his friends—hiking and camping, swimming and dreaming. Now, as an artist, he came to this same world of woods and mountains to search out places that had been cultivated and bred in his imagination and embedded in his subconscious all his life. Buried in him was this sense of place and now, with the eyes and mind of a painter, he tried to give visual form to what he felt was the spirit and character of his countryside, merging and enlivening it with what he always referred to as his "temperament," a quality he deemed is always found in all serious art.

On previous visits to this site, he had worked out the particular motif he wanted to paint this day. He located himself at the place where his view of the rocks and trees and the intervals between them came together into the precise configuration he desired. In the clear bright light, he scrutinized the sharply defined shadow patterns; the way they impacted the forms before him was crucial to his composition. While some of the shadows clarified the forms they fell across, others obscured the contours and caused certain planes to seem to merge.

Once, when he paused to look off into the surrounding countryside, there arose a long-forgotten memory of himself with his two childhood friends, Émile Zola and Baptistin Baille, roaming over these very hills that surrounded him now. Ever together in those early school years, their friendship almost had the force of a sacred pact among the three. When they were not swimming, fishing, or hiking, they argued what they thought were the great artistic issues of the day or else read to one another from works by their favorite authors and poets of the moment. They dreamed of going forth one day themselves to conquer the twin worlds of art and literature.

Cézanne smiled as he recalled a particular incident during one of these outings when they camped not far from the very place where he now stood. He had climbed to the top of a great rock, and from the high perch it provided above his friends, he recited in a loud, declamatory voice some long passage or other from…was it Victor Hugo's *Hernani*? He could not recall. But he remembered the shouting and the clapping from his attentive audience of two when he finished.

Shifting his weight as a small rock beneath his left foot moved, his mind snapped back to the present. *Whatever made me think of all that? How odd,* he wondered to himself.

The sight of the rocks and trees before him reclaimed his attention, and he resumed the task of organizing himself for the morning's work. Because of the steepness of the hillside, an unusual amount of time was required to set up. The easel had to be adjusted to the severe and uneven incline, and since a careless misstep could result in a fall, the position of his feet needed to be carefully thought out and tested. His perch here among the rocks was restricted and uncomfortable, but neither factor bothered him much. At least in these circumstances he was sure that no one would disturb him.

This comforting thought had hardly crossed his mind when he heard below the sounds of dried pine needles crunching underfoot and tiny pebbles rolling and falling. A glance downward confirmed his worst fear.

Climbing unsteadily over the rocks below him was an elderly man of about Cézanne's own age. Unsure of foot, this person reached out awkwardly to grasp any support available—nearby rocky ledges, limbs of trees, clumps of brush. He held a cane, which he sometimes hooked over his forearm when he needed both hands or used to keep his balance at other times. Once, in order to pull himself up, he tried without success to hook its curved end around the branch of a slender tree.

This seemingly intrepid gentleman was dressed in a manner quite unsuited for the task or the weather. He wore a bowler hat, just like one Cézanne himself often wore, and a black suit with a long coat. The artist owned such a suit, a style and type much favored by the reserved and elderly gentlemen of Aix. When this tall, thin man started his climb, his stiff white shirt was buttoned tightly at the collar.

As he mounted the steep incline, the artist could plainly see a long, angular face framed by a moustache and goatee, both similar to his own and just as white. Once when the man's hat fell off, there appeared a head every bit as bald as the painter's own. Two strands of a string tie fluttered and twisted in the air.

Halfway up the incline, the stranger paused to wipe his brow with a large white handkerchief. The heat was taking its toll. Then he carefully refolded the handkerchief before returning it to its place in his coat pocket. Before starting out again, he took off his coat and unbuttoned his shirt collar. But when he resumed climbing, he found he needed both hands, and this forced him to put his coat back on.

Too tense to enjoy the comic side of all these actions, the artist could only stand mute and dumbfounded. As the man struggled upward toward him, the painter wavered between wanting to offer assistance and crying out in anger at this intrusion. In this uncharacteristic state of indecision, he neither helped nor protested but simply stood watching.

With shirt collar undone and dust all over his clothing, the stranger came abreast of Cézanne. The space where they stood was so confining they could hardly stand together without touching. The stranger sweated and breathed heavily. At least now he could relieve himself of his coat, which he held in one hand. Without speaking, he took off his hat and used it, as best he could, to fan himself. Then he looked around, chose a moderately sloping rock, and approached it with an unsteady step. Now at least there was a little distance separating the two men. Precarious though his position was on the sloping face of the huge boulder, the stranger for the moment remained standing.

The painter maintained his odd silence through all these maneuvers. He spoke not a word but stared incredulously. He could not take his eyes off this man. Although he could not say why, this odd person exerted a peculiar fascination for him.

After once more wiping his brow, the stranger finally elected to speak and in a disgruntled tone said, "Cézanne, you do find the oddest places to paint. And in this awful heat. Look at my clothes."

He held up his coat, shaking it, while trying to brush some of the dust from his trousers with his free hand. Making little progress, he spoke up again with a voice still more irritated. "What can there possibly be up here on this absurd precipice that you can't find in a more comfortable setting on flatter ground? To stand here all day, you must be part goat."

Without waiting for an answer, the stranger instead occupied himself with getting more comfortable. Looking around, he located a suitable place to sit. He set his cane and hat to one side and refolded his coat. But before laying it across a nearby rock, he reached into an inside pocket, from which he produced a small silver flask. Unscrewing the top, he drank off a small quantity of its contents.

"I was with the Countess de Lubersac the day before yesterday," the stranger said, his voice becoming suddenly chatty and sociable. "Her villa in Cannes, you know. Such a charming place. Wonderful gardens. Before I left, the dear thing was kind enough to let me refill my little supply here with some of her best reserve."

He patted the flask with obvious satisfaction and then gestured to Cézanne to share some of the cognac with him. "Aged the full twenty-five years." He paused a moment and then added,

"She assured me. Here, have some."

The stranger leaned forward, extending his arm toward the painter. Then he abruptly pulled the flask back. "No, no, you shouldn't, should you. Of course not. How stupid of me. Your diabetes and all."

The stranger shrugged, withdrew his arm, screwed down the cap, and returned the metal container to its place in the pocket of his coat. Then in the most relaxed and easy manner, he leaned back, put his hands behind his head, crossed one leg over the other and, smiling, said matter-of-factly, "Well, this certainly isn't the Boboli Gardens, is it?"

That did it; the painter erupted. Pointing a finger at the stranger, Cézanne shouted, "Who are you?" Then, taking a deep breath, he yelled, "I don't know you!" And finally, throwing his arms up in exasperation, he cried, "Shit!"

Cézanne picked up a twig off the ground and hurled it back down again. It pinged off a rock and made a little puff of dust as it landed at the feet of the stranger.

"Get hold of yourself," replied the stranger calmly. "I'm only trying to make the point that, at my age, I don't belong up here hanging off the side of a cliff like a mountaineer, and you don't either. At this late time in our lives, both of us should be enjoying the comforts of more benign surroundings. Someplace less coarse, less dangerous; someplace more refined…more…"

"This is where I work!" snapped the artist. "My motif is here."

"Nonsense. There are a thousand places more comfortable than this that are just as interesting to paint. You have chosen this precarious spot because of your absurd obsession about working where you won't be intruded upon. Admit it. Really, it's so ridiculous, dear fellow."

"That's not true," shot back the artist. "But if it were, it didn't do me much good, did it?" Cézanne glared at this strange man whose intrusion now began to deeply annoy him. "And stop talking to me as if you know me," the artist said. "I've never seen you before in my life. Who are you? A painter? A collector? More like a meddler! Who told you how to find me? Who was it?"

The stranger calmly replied, "Who I am is of no importance. I'm certainly not an artist, at least not as you think of an artist. As for a collector..." He paused. "What an amusing idea. I have never thought of it like that. Why, yes," the stranger laughed weirdly, "you might say I'm a collector of preposterous ambitions and impossible dreams!"

Cézanne shuddered, wondering if he were alone on this steep hillside with someone mentally unbalanced.

With a certain excitement mounting in his voice, the stranger said, "Think of me as someone who takes an interest in eccentric and excessive behavior. I am drawn to people who hopelessly flail away at some outlandish ambition far beyond their capacities. Especially those who spend years at it, like yourself. You are among those strange, delusional people who throw yourselves away on senseless endeavors and grind your lives to dust with unrewarded labor. I am drawn to such persons as you whose dreams are far beyond your capabilities. It's perverse of me, I know, but people like you absolutely intrigue me. I find what you inflict upon yourself endlessly interesting."

Cézanne could not believe what he was hearing. He had never before laid eyes on this preposterous man who nevertheless spoke to him as if he knew him intimately.

The artist suddenly felt cornered. Here in a place he had chosen himself, and which he now wished were not so confining, he wondered how he could extricate himself from this absurd situation. The stranger, meanwhile, went on as if there were complete understanding between them.

"I once had a disease, myself, like yours," he said. "It was an ambition out of all proportion to my abilities. In my youth there was something I thought I truly longed to do, but after a certain period of sustained effort, including lessons, I saw it was no use. I could not make the ultimate commitment. I had neither the strength nor the talent, I guess. Others even told me I could never become first-rate. I don't know, I just could not find my way to carry on. Certainly the world ignored my efforts, just as it does yours. When I finally realized I could not achieve anything of significance, I came to my senses. I did the most obvious and rational thing: I gave up."

In the course of delivering these stark words, the stranger had risen to his feet, putting the two men on the same level, eye to eye. They stared at each other, the artist with a pained look on his face; the other, his head slightly tipped up, a half smile around his lips.

Seeing that the artist continued his silence, the stranger launched again into what was becoming a harangue. "To me, it makes no sense for a person to voluntarily suffer as much pain as you do for no reward or recognition. In fact it drives me crazy. Cézanne, to others you must see that you look like a fool. Just think about it. Isn't it imbecilic that you continue so late in life this unrewarded quest in art? God knows you work hard enough, but look around you. With few exceptions, nobody knows or cares about what you paint. If they do look, it's to laugh not praise."

Now the stranger pulled back somewhat. It worried him that he may have gone too far in his criticism of the painter. But

Cézanne remained unexpectedly silent, only his stern look betraying what might be rising anger. The artist's silence encouraged the stranger to make one more effort at reaching him. He spoke again, slowly and with emphasis, seeming to have reached some point of importance that he needed to convey to Cézanne.

"Most interesting of all is this—and listen to me carefully—in an instant you can be free of this great burden you have carried all these years. Think of it, you can put your brushes down! To do that lies fully within your power, though you act like it does not. You imagine that you must paint, that your life is not worth living otherwise. But is that really so? You can stop painting and take your ease at any time and, as I said, who will care? Who will miss what you do not paint? And meanwhile, you will be spared so much mental anguish and bodily fatigue. You have no obligations and plenty of money. You can indulge any whim. But of course you won't, and that fascinates me."

In spite of increasing feelings of uneasiness, Cézanne finally answered back with great feeling. "These words you speak are asinine. You describe a life of idleness and self-indulgence as if it were some form of higher existence. If such is your choice, then we have chosen to live in directly opposite ways. Your words have nothing to do with me. You don't know anything about me. Go away. Find someone else to bother. Stop wasting my time."

In response the stranger stubbornly sat down again. He leaned back against a sloping stone and threw his arms apart in a careless, defiant manner. The whole movement of his body conveyed determination as well as disdain, and it made Cézanne all the more uncomfortable. "Believe me, I've gone to a lot of trouble to learn about you," the stranger went on. "You're an especially interesting study for me, one of the best I've come across. Not as good as van Gogh, of course; you haven't gone that far…at least not yet. He knew no limits either. He was even crazier than you! He threw himself into painting like a log into fire, and the outcome was perfectly predictable: he burned himself to ashes."

The smile on the stranger's face made a grisly contrast to the meaning of his words.

The painter looked away. Then he bent down as if he would pick up the pouch that held his paints and brushes.

"There's not much about you I don't know," the stranger continued, paying no attention to the painter's tentative movements to pack up his things. "My investigations are most thorough. When I take on a project like you, I feel I almost become you. Or haven't you noticed?"

These remarks brought Cézanne, who had been squatting next to his painting equipment, up on his feet. From this position he looked down at this person who more and more antagonized him. With a grin, the stranger, stroking his white goatee, looked up at the painter. The artist thought to himself, *He's mad. I'm up here alone with a madman.*

Feigning a weak smile of his own, the painter stalled for time. "Then you're an artist?"

"No, no, not that. I don't paint," replied the stranger. "I don't need to do that. I am a collector of facts."

Cézanne uttered a groan.

"To me, your life is an open book." The stranger held out one hand, palm up. "And what desperate and uninformed choices lie within its pages. What missed opportunities! If I may say so, your life is a maze of wrong turns. At least when van Gogh took up painting, he was without anything to lose because at that point in his life he had nothing. But you, my friend, with the support of your banker-father, had everything."

"My father? You speak to me of him? Did you know my father?"

"No, not personally. We never actually spoke, but I knew him. Oh, I knew and admired him. I watched him over the years, and I heard him. He was amazing to behold. Unstinting in his devotion to his business, he had an unerring ability to size up any client wishing to borrow his money. He rarely made a mistake. No one got past him. He always made a return on his money and then some. And as you know, he made lots of it."

The stranger's face was ringed by a gleeful smile.

"What are you talking about?" asked the painter, more perplexed than ever by what he was hearing. "How could you have watched and heard him for years if you did not meet him...if you did not speak to him? You are not making any sense. You are talking gibberish"

"Never mind," said the stranger. "Just know that I knew him to be what he was: a superb businessman who achieved great success and who would have sponsored you in any respectable endeavor you wished. Why, to have left the crowning achievement of his life—his bank—in your hands would have pleased him beyond anything else."

Cézanne shook his head and let his hunched-over body slide to the ground.

"But what did you choose?" cried the stranger. "Art! A life fraught with such uncertainty and difficulty, a profession so marginal and unsavory, a way so filled with frustration and despair, that it was a choice beyond belief for anyone in your enviable circumstances. But at this point I need not tell you, eh?"

In an effort to ignore the stranger's oppressive tirade, the painter went back to his original question and asked, "How could you know these things about my father if you never met him? I don't believe you. You are making all this up. I know you didn't know him. I never saw you in my father's company. You don't know anything about my father."

"I can understand your saying that," replied the stranger. "But you spent so little time with him, how would you know who was in his company? When he was alive, you would go to any lengths to avoid him. Basically, you were terrified of him. Or, if you had to be in his presence, you did anything to placate him, except in the only thing he ever really wanted you to do: take up a decent profession."

Suddenly angry, Cézanne raised his voice. "You bring all that up now? My taking up the law? Banking? That was so many years ago. Why, that was over thirty years ago! What can you possibly know about that? Besides, it was my life, my responsibility to choose my own life. It was not his right to…"

The artist started coughing. The sudden rush of anger taxed him terribly. His face grew red; his breath came in gasps. He felt faint.

The stranger, startled by his fury, became alarmed. "Now look what you have done. You must calm yourself. You shouldn't waste your energy on such a senseless outburst. Your health is delicate enough as it is. You'll be exhausted tonight and have one of those dreadful nightmarish sleeps. Tomorrow you'll be perfectly useless and probably grumpy besides. Get a grip on yourself."

When the spasm passed, the artist went on about his father. "I could never make him understand. I never knew what to say to him. He never cared about what I was trying to do…"

Once more the stranger interrupted abruptly, bursting forth in a long, full-throated laugh. "Oh, that's perfect! It's exactly what I mean. You should hear yourself: 'He didn't understand what I was trying to do.' That's really very amusing. Listen to me: does anyone even now—these many years later—understand what you are trying to do? Is there a living soul, after all this time, who knows or cares about what you are trying to do? You persist in making pictures that baffle everyone who looks at them. For decades now you have thrown your life away in the manufacture of things that only bring down upon you scorn, ridicule, and pain. It's absurd. You must see that."

The stranger was becoming very agitated. The artist's reluctance to accept or even acknowledge any of his points was maddening.

He tried again. "How many times have you said so yourself, 'Not even Pissarro understands? Not even Monet?' You have worked for years sacrificing everything—friends, pleasures, even your health. How often do you come home from the studio so exhausted you can't eat? You have all you can do sometimes just to get into bed where you have, at best, only a fitful, unsatisfying sleep. Unfit for human companionship, you live by yourself for weeks and months on end, letting no one near you. You are dissatisfied with everything you do. Tortured. Depressed. I can't believe the number of works you have destroyed or abandoned, as if possessed by some demon that drives you to a standard beyond what is possible. You strive for some unrealizable perfection—to you, no doubt, a vision. What you call your 'sensations.' Fantasy, I say. Delusion!"

The expression of amazement on Cézanne's face caught the stranger's attention. "Look at you now. You think I'm insane," said the stranger. "You think you are stranded up here alone with a madman. But who are you, living and working as you do, to call someone else crazy!"

Suddenly the artist, with newfound firmness in his voice,

cried out, "Stop this now! How dare you speak to me this way? Who are you to say these things to me?"

The stranger, speaking rapidly, interrupted again. "No, no. You don't understand. You are not listening to me. Think about what I'm saying. After all this time and effort, where are you in your career? What kind of recognition have you achieved? You are a joke at the Academy."

The stranger suddenly raised his voice. He began shouting. The thought of Cézanne's persistence all these years in the face of repeated failure and rejection enraged him. "So why go on? Can't you see how pointless it is? You are old. Give it over. Give it up…"

The stranger's face grew red. Raising his arms in a gesture of despair, his words came forth in a gasp. "…like I did!"

The artist stepped back, amazed and frightened, at this sudden outburst. He almost fell but caught his balance. The stranger sat for several minutes shaking and unable to speak. Then, as he calmed himself somewhat, he looked hard again at the painter, and continued his rambling fulminations. "What brings me here at just this time is your latest folly, absolutely the worst decision you have ever made. I'm speaking about this exhibition at Vollard's. It's madness!"

The mention of the art dealer's name caught Cézanne by surprise. "Monsieur Vollard? My exhibition with him? What do you know about that? You know nothing about that. Nobody knows anything about that except Monsieur Vollard, my son, and me."

"You are quite wrong; many people know. Word is spreading quickly," said the stranger.

"But I just agreed to do this only three days ago," said Cézanne, looking tired and confused.

Ignoring the artist's consternation, the stranger kept at him. "What possesses you? What makes you think there's an audience of anyone significant out there now, when before there was none? You have held back so many years, working almost in secret. Why risk it all now? Can't you see how horrible it will be? The public will come down on you with all its might. Or else it will ignore you altogether. Either way, it will be a disaster. You must be tired. It's time to stop. Although you will not listen, I am here to say to you that you must stop using up your life in this impossible enterprise. For your own sake, enjoy the little time you have left in peace and rest. To do otherwise is folly. Persistence is a virtue only when the objective is obtainable."

Cézanne was astounded by the vehemence of the stranger. How could this fellow know these things? He seemed to know Monet and Pissarro. Had they told him? Had Vollard? No, that was absurd. Angry as he felt at these insults, he was also gripped by a certain fascination. No one before had ever said these things to his face.

The stranger stared intently at the painter, reading his face and eyes for reactions. Again he wondered if he had gone too far. He knew that Cézanne had the power to end this encounter instantly, simply by leaving. Surely his purpose had been to test the artist and feed his insecurities, not drive him away.

Cézanne sat perfectly still, looking past the stranger, lost in some private meditation. Finally he reached out and removed the canvas from the easel.

"You're leaving?"

"Yes."

"Why?"

"That should be obvious. It's impossible now for me to work. You insist on thrusting yourself upon me. My concentration is broken. I am tired. I must leave."

"No, no, don't go! Not yet! Not before we've finished our discussion…" The stranger reached out toward the artist as if to grab his arm.

"Don't touch me!" the old artist said as he threw out his arm and brushed aside the stranger's extended hand. "We cannot possibly have anything more to discuss."

The artist leaned the small blank canvas against a stone and started to break down the folding easel.

"You know, it wasn't Hugo that day. It was de Musset."

"What day?" asked Cézanne distractedly, his mind still filled with thoughts stirred by the stranger's wild speech.

"The day you recited to Émile and Baptistin from that rock near here. You got the summers mixed up. Victor Hugo was your hero the year before. That summer it was Alfred de Musset. You recited lines from *The Nights*."

With satisfaction, the stranger watched Cézanne's body stiffen.

In a state of amazement, the artist thought to himself, *My God, now he's reading my mind, and he's right: it was Alfred de Musset! But how can he know that? How can he know what I was thinking just before he climbed up here? It's such a silly thing to know. Nobody could know from which book I was reciting except Émile, Baptistin, and me. Nobody!*

Addressing the stranger, he said, "So you know Émile? You know Baptistin?"

"I knew Zola a long time ago when he was young and just starting out," the stranger replied. "Did he never speak to you about me? I found him attractive then, when he was destitute, desperate, and full of wild literary ambitions. I loved following him around then. But not long after, he began having some success and I lost interest in him. But to answer your question: no, it wasn't he who told me about you standing on that rock reciting poetry. It wasn't Baille either."

The artist dropped his easel and stood stiffly, his anger and frustration in full possession of him again. "One of them must have told you, dammit! There's no other way you could know that. No one else was there."

"Look at you. You are furious again."

In an agonized voice, the artist shot back, "Then you read it in Émile's book about me."

"*The Masterpiece?* No, it's not in there either. Zola did not mention that incident there. Besides, that story of his is not about you. You do Zola such injustice. His hero in that novel is as much Manet as he is you. And some of Courbet and himself thrown in. And probably others, as well. So what if at the end of the book Claude Lantier commits suicide? He kills himself not as a comment on you and your friends but because the story compels it. How could that be you?"

The painter looked down and did not answer. The stranger went on, "And after you read his book, you wrote Zola that curt note and have never written or spoken to him again. Nearly ten years of silence after how many...forty...years of friendship? What a pity. And all the things he did for you, your oldest and best friend."

"So you think that's all it was, eh?" replied Cézanne hotly. "And you who claim to know everything about me. Well, before that book was even written, what was left of our friendship? What was really there besides the memories of old times past? In the end we had nothing between us that was alive and ongoing. We really had little or nothing to say to each other, nothing of importance to share. His life and mine had taken such different turnings. He moved in that uppity society where I never felt comfortable or welcome. That huge house, his estate at Médan, always packed with such fancy guests. Oh, he tried to keep me around. He always invited me, and for a while I enjoyed it, but I never really fit in. All the literati, the politicians. I was happiest when he'd let me go off somewhere alone in his gardens or along the river with my paints. Besides, my work never meant anything to him. He never had the faintest idea about what I was trying to do. Our break was long in coming; finally it was no use, our friendship had become no more than a meaningless habit…a dried-out husk."

Cézanne's words trailed off so that they were barely audible. Speaking and thinking were becoming more difficult for him. He was feeling increasingly tired and confused.

But with seeming insensitivity to the artist's distress, the stranger continued. "You must admit that in the old days Zola fired off some great salvos on behalf of you, your colleagues, and the new painting. Need I remind you of all those newspaper articles defending you against all your critics?"

Cézanne looked up from where he had again seated himself. "Yes, he did all that. When we needed a voice to face down the mob, Émile was always there. He roared like a lion, didn't he? Of course we had to feed him the things to say. Poor Émile never did know what a painting really was. He always thought it was just another form of literature. But that didn't matter, at least not at first. He may not have known much about art, but he knew the politics of the underdog! How he snarled at them, eh? And they all reared back and took notice."

At these thoughts of former times, the old artist's face brightened for a moment. Then a sadness replaced the smile and turned quickly to irritation as he said, "I hate writers on art; I hate them all!"

"Even Balzac and Baudelaire?" asked the stranger, smiling.

"You do know a thing or two about me, don't you? No, not Balzac or Baudelaire; I do not hate them. But only them! Just those two may write about art, do you hear? No one else."

Cézanne stared in defiance at the stranger, who tossed his head back and laughed once again. "Well, that commandment should be easy to carry out. Balzac and Baudelaire are both dead! As for those still living, however, it's a different story. If your edict were to hold, there would be a lot of disappointed writers around here if they couldn't practice their craft. What about Duret? What about Rivière and Huysmans? What about your young friend Émile Bernard?"

"Him especially!" cried Cézanne. "He drove me crazy with his infernal questions when he was here. He wanted to unscrew the top of my skull to look directly into my brain! He wants my opinion on absolutely everything. He still hounds me in the letters he writes. My paintings are my statements. Aren't they enough?"

"Oh, really, Cézanne," continued the stranger in this seemingly conciliatory tone. "I was much too harsh when I spoke before. There are, after all, young people who like what you do. Émile Bernard deeply admires your work, and so do his friends. These young people are your main support. You have no idea how fiercely they defend your painting to anyone who criticizes it. You shouldn't be so close-minded. You shouldn't be so ungrateful. You should be less..."

"Stop judging me!" cried out the artist.

Cézanne had risen to his feet again, his arms spread and his fists clenched. The stranger's words and tone had gone back to the accusatory qualities that characterized his earlier inventory of the artist's supposed faults and failures. Like cues in a play, these latest reproaches alerted Cézanne, and he suddenly remembered that he was still talking to someone who had not even identified himself yet who presumptuously imposed himself on the artist in the most outrageous way. It was so unlike the painter to tolerate even a fraction of such behavior from anyone, especially a person he did not know. The stranger was diabolical in the ways he found to keep him engaged, but now it was over. This conversation must stop.

"Who are you? Tell me your name. You do have a name?" Cézanne's voice was thick with sarcasm.

"Ah, yes, my name. You can't be content until you have a name, can you? But what will telling you my name accomplish? You don't know it; you don't know me. It won't mean a thing. I might as well tell you that I'm Baldassare—Count Baldassare Castiglione. Now there was somebody worth knowing, somebody to be. Yes, if you must have a name, call me Baldassare."

Pleased with himself, the stranger smiled while the artist scowled. Ignoring Cézanne's disapproving look, the stranger went on. "He epitomizes all that is grand and eloquent in a gentleman. He was a great and generous nobleman, a model of his age. You know, of course, Raphael's portrait of him in the Louvre. Raphael caught all his best qualities in that brilliant painting. A man who knew how to live! You should look into the count's life; he has things to teach you. Read his book on manners. What refinements of taste, even when shunning all excesses. He had many pursuits, unlike you. He was not fixated. He was the model of the Roman society of his day, a friend and patron of great artists, a truly…"

"What kind of devious, insolent answer is this?" shouted the artist. "You mock me. You take too much for granted. Damn your Baldassare Castiglione!"

As he paused in thought, he muttered, "I'll play your game." Slowly the scowl on the artist's face faded. "I have it. You are Ratapoil!"

A moment passed as the stranger digested Cézanne's choice for a name.

"Me?" said the stranger, frowning, "Daumier's Ratapoil? How can you?"

Cézanne was suddenly quite pleased with himself, especially as the stranger grew more agitated. "Compare me to him?" cried the stranger. "How insulting! Now it is you who have gone too far."

"Not at all," returned the artist. "Ratapoil was a thief, a wretch, a liar, and a whole lot more. You steal my time, you thief. You make ill of my efforts, you wretch. And you are far less than honest with me, you liar. The way you have imposed yourself on me is utterly lacking in good manners, and that also comports well with Ratapoil."

The stranger's silence seemed to acknowledge the standoff. "It's time to bring this interview to a close," he finally said. "You look exhausted. Sometime soon we will meet again to continue our discussion in a more sanguine state of mind. Also, I trust, in more comfortable surroundings. Perhaps your studio, eh?"

The artist bristled. "What? Another interview? You will come again? I must talk to you again? In my studio? No! Never! You will never come to me again. I only want to be left alone. I must have my privacy. The world is a frightening place, and I am endowed neither with the strength nor the cunning to survive in it. And I will not have you subjecting me to more of your interviews and discussions. No more interviews! No more discussions!"

Cézanne rose unsteadily to his feet, holding the easel and canvas awkwardly in one hand. With the other he picked up the pouch containing the paints and brushes. The bag had not even been opened. He stood there for a moment, glaring at this infuriating man who sat calmly looking back at him. Without speaking a word, he began with unsteady steps the descent of the steep incline—canvas, easel, and bag all swaying oddly.

As the painter got partway down the hill, the stranger could hear him talking loudly to himself, saying, "No, absolutely not. No more interviews. No more questions. No more talk. I just want to be left alone."

The stranger watched the painter slowly make his way safely to the bottom of the hill. Without so much as a glance backward, the old artist turned and disappeared around a corner of the Château Noir.

4

Mont Sainte-Victoire from the Quarry

For Cézanne painting was a form of meditation, and the wooded countryside around Aix-en-Provence was one of his favorite subjects for contemplation. The stands of pine trees—interspersed with sycamores, oaks, and cypresses—framed the outcroppings of the rocky cliffs and narrow ledges common to these hillsides. His preferred views often contained patches of blue sky above and the characteristic reddish earth below, both appearing as if filtered through a mesh of crisscrossing branches hung with rhythmically layered foliage. Depending upon his angle of view, the tree trunks marked off the landscape in vibrant intervals of space, like brackets in some mysterious punctuation. For years he had diligently studied this complex syntax, locating in it any number of his precious motifs.

When he mounted the crests of certain hills where the trees parted and vistas unfolded, Cézanne could take in with equal zest the wider, deeper panoramas. From these various vantage points he saw Mont Sainte-Victoire, the grand mountain to the east of Aix whose scale and distinctive shape commanded the admiration of inhabitant and visitor alike.

In a gradual process that spanned years, he was drawn more

and more to this mountain as subject for his art. Painting this imposing object had become an obsession in recent years.

In his early efforts to depict the mountain, he mostly chose wide views with a deep axis into the depth of the landscape. From across the Arc River his motif centered on how the mountain came together with the valley. He searched out the nearly imperceptible transitions by which the gentle sides of the valley blended almost invisibly into the wall of the mountain, making one uninterrupted whole.

This piece of rock, so physically dense and enduring, was yet visually so changeable when seen from different perspectives and distances. To the north of the city, from the top of a hill called Les Lauves, where his studio was located, the mountain's craggy mass rising grandly on the horizon above tree-studded fields was a spectacular sight. From here, an intervening plain cut sharply across the mountain's base, letting it appear to rise abruptly from the level plateau. The great crown of rock seemed free of its terrestrial underpinnings, as if floating in grand and solitary isolation.

In response to this different set of visual conditions, the painter found himself reversing what he had done before. Instead of pulling the mountain and the valley together in a single, flawless unity, he worked to dramatize this feeling of separation between the soaring rock and its foundation. In several of his recent canvases, the mountain appeared as some mysterious vessel majestically gliding across a sea of swirling greens and earthy browns.

Another set of motifs coming from his study of Mont Sainte-Victoire was more varied and therefore harder to define. These variations involved the juxtaposition of the mountain with something nearby. Sometimes he painted clumps of trees with the mountain surging above them or with trunks and foliage framing the far-off peak. Two versions of Sainte-Victoire were sited with the road to the tiny village of Le Tholonet below it, the narrow route flanked by umbrella pines. Or sometimes he set the mountain alongside a farm building or with the Château Noir placed to one side. This latter building, where he often painted and sometimes stayed, was a large house on a property between Aix and the mountain.

On this particular day, Cézanne planned to continue work on a view of the mountain rising above the cliffs in the abandoned rock quarry called Bibémus. Located on a ridge above the Château Noir, this quarry had supplied most of the stones used in the previous century to build the stately mansions lining the Cours Mirabeau in Aix, but it had been abandoned for as long as Cézanne could remember.

The men who had worked this quarry, now long gone, left behind the chiseled remnants of decades of labor. Scattered everywhere throughout the tree-strewn hill, sculpted masses of vertically cut stone in random formations gave parts of the landscape an architectural cast. These carved geometries set against the rawer, more natural rock were particularly fascinating and exciting to Cézanne, who found in them numerous motifs to inspire him. And besides the great beauty of the place, the old artist loved the isolation there. He could work for days on end without encountering another human being.

He had spent the night in the old stone cabin in the quarry precinct, a one-room structure he had been renting since coming to Bibémus to work. He used it occasionally as a convenient place to stay for a night or two during periods of good weather when, as now, he was working on paintings here in the quarry. In spite of the quarry's nearness to the city, it was rarely visited.

The place where he wanted to paint this morning was not far away, but he decided on a little side excursion before going to his painting site. He walked to the edge of the quarry area where there were fields and occasional farm buildings. He went to a place that had recently caught his attention for its potential as a subject for a new painting. Looking for new places to work was a regular part of his routine, and the selection of a site was not a quick or spontaneous act on his part because the commitment to it could occupy him for long periods.

Two closely spaced clumps of sycamores on the edge of an open field framed a pair of farm buildings in the distance. Two long, slender branches—both emanating from the largest tree on his left—reached horizontally across the space to the group of trees on the right. Passing a little above his eye level, these sinuous boughs, like two thick lines in space, made an arresting midair configuration. Running close together and more or less parallel, the two limbs crossed and then recrossed each other at two points along their paths. These intersections formed a pointed ellipse in the air, through which the artist could see one of the distant farm buildings.

As so often occurred in his choice of sites to paint, the precise place where he stood was crucial to the effect he sought. Sometimes just one step in either direction could seriously compromise or change the relationship between elements in the composition. In this case, just a small shift of position would move the distant farm building outside of the elliptical "eye" of intersecting branches.

The precision with which these branches framed the three windows of the upper story of the left-hand building intrigued him. The elliptical arrangement of the branches linked the foreground and background. He thought of the composition as parallel planes, the two groups of trees in the foreground making up the front plane, and the buildings behind, with their own trees and bushes, forming the second one. The open field between, as well as the shallow depression in which the trees grew, formed the lower, intermediate planes.

By a single step to his right, he caused the scene before him to rearrange itself. From this altered position, both buildings moved to the right of the two clumps of trees and fell outside of the elliptical window formed by the intersecting branches. The opening now looked into empty blue sky and the farmhouses, pushed to the right, aligned themselves more fully with the right-hand group of trees. The first arrangement seemed to call for a balanced, symmetrical disposition of parts, the farmhouse held in the "eye" of the curving branches at the center. A more dynamic possibility presented itself in the second arrangement, the right-hand clump of trees fusing with the houses behind to become the main focus.

The better choice between these two compositions was not yet readily apparent to Cézanne. Both were very interesting, so he resolved to come back again; eventually one of the views would take precedence. It occurred to him that in the autumn there might be an even more intriguing situation after the leaves had fallen. Numerous smaller branches in the foreground trees, hard to see now, would be more visible, making a pronounced network of spaces across the background landscape, pulling everything together even more.

But now it was time to get to his site in the quarry. The morning sun was approaching the angle he desired.

The painting Cézanne brought with him on this morning was already well advanced, having been the object of numerous work sessions over a period of several weeks. "Well advanced" was, however, such a relative term, as he persistently painted over and over canvases that to others would have long since seemed completed. But at each succeeding session, the direct contact with nature usually brought forth some new perception or relationship that he found necessary to incorporate into his work. It was as if every act of painting were simultaneously a new act of seeing and as if the seeing itself were an endless reaching out to ever-shifting contexts of form and color. With brush in hand, the immediacy of the thing beheld—the object or setting in direct contact with his senses—always seemed capable of disclosing itself in newer, deeper, and more subtle ways.

Because of this nearly interminable circumstance, the painting process usually ended by his stopping work on a canvas, not finishing it. Exhaustion or frustration were the main reasons he abandoned so many paintings. In any case, the canvas he planned to work on now had already undergone several transformations and would undoubtedly go through more of them. He had long ago become resigned to this process.

Although he had painted this painting over and over, there were still parts left bare, the canvas itself untouched. It was not uncommon to find these tiny areas of unpainted canvas in his work. Often these bare spaces were so small and discreet they did not hinder anyone's appreciation of the work as a whole. These unfinished parts were often so subtle in their character that years later some admirers of his work would claim he had intentionally left them there. But he thought of these open areas as passages he was so far unable to complete. Once, when explaining this problem, he had made a gesture of slowly interlocking fingers of both his hands as a way of describing how carefully and completely the tonalities of his patches of color had to come together. He declared that if even one of these passages was out of control, it would negatively affect the whole canvas, forcing him in the worst case to repaint the entire work.

As was his custom, he arrived at the site before the light had reached the point appropriate for his painting. This matter of the light, especially in a landscape setting, was always such a devilish and elusive problem. His sensitivity to light and color, cultivated over years of disciplined seeing, made almost any return to a place of work into something new or something more. The very quality of the air on a given day could bring differences in his response to what he saw, and often these differences needed to be incorporated into the painting, sometimes changing it radically. Keeping his painting in harmony with what he saw during each work session was the critical piece in his process, and due to the nature of the subtle changes always occurring in the subject before him, his painting had to be dynamic in its response to those changes.

The site he had chosen for this painting was in itself dramatic, and that drama was pushed to the utmost in the particular view he had selected. He stood along one side of a narrow ravine looking across at two low cliffs separated by a narrow gap of space. The tops of both cliffs that flanked the gap were rounded and stood a little above the horizontal line of the rest of the cliff wall. Their rounded tops appeared like a pair of domed sentinels flanking the opening between them, through which grass and trees could be seen.

These two rocky formations had almost certainly once been joined in one continuous wall of stone, but many decades before, when the quarry was an active enterprise, workers shaped them into their present form and forced the opening between them. The exposed surfaces of stone were now dry and bleached from years of assault by the hot sun and the fierce winds of the

Mistral. To what was left behind, the subsequent years of sun, wind, and rain had put the finishing touches, rounding the edges and smoothing the surfaces.

This was a compelling project of man and nature together that gave these stone faces a quasi-architectural character. Like giant newel posts, side by side, their rounded tops gently curved aboveground while their straight sides joined the wall of the ravine. The two rock formations dropped vertically to a lower sloping tier of earth where a scattering of small pine trees grew, their long needles rising up in discreet, sharply defined masses against the sheer cliffs.

Most striking, though, was the color of the stone, ochre and sienna with strong touches of rusty red and burnt orange. This distinctive coloration was characteristic of the region immediately around Aix, largely the result of certain ferrous deposits in the earth.

Within the rectangle of the canvas, Cézanne had set all this elaborate geological structure into the lower two-thirds of his composition. The narrow gap between the knobs of rock was slightly to the right of center and the wall of the ravine more extensive to the left. But all of this was only the foundation for the rest of the painting.

This low-slung escarpment was the springboard for a momentous view of Mont Sainte-Victoire soaring above it. The space above the rocky ridge was filled with the powerful body of the mountain. The upward angle of view was such that one's eye went from the top of the nearby wall of rock directly to the great mass of the mountain with no visible terrain intervening. The mountain was actually several kilometers away from where he stood. Only because of the particular angle at which he viewed things was he able to imagine the mountain as hovering over the ravine cliff.

This particular viewing situation was at the heart of the motif—the nearby ravine and the distant mountain brought dramatically together. In the painting the real distance between them disappeared, with the bare rock of the mountain seeming to come down directly onto the ledge of the ravine wall!

He wanted to preserve and express this unique visual juxtaposition in the strongest possible terms. He wanted to paint it as forcefully as it appeared to his eye, unmediated as much as possible by other cognitive knowledge of the situation. To stress his point to the utmost, he even enlarged the mountain to further diminish the sense of distance between it and the low cliffs in the foreground.

From years of looking and thinking about what he looked at, he had come to realize that seeing involves choices of the most complex kind. Whether randomly or with purpose, we choose the objects we see from the multitude of things around us; therefore our choosing is crucial to what we see.

The very choice of landscape here was daring and full of subversion of the old optics. The relationship between the foreground and background planes was anticlassical in the extreme. The abrupt leap in space from the ravine to the mountain in this painting lay at the core of his radical vision. For centuries in traditional landscape painting, the near and the far were most often brought together by subtle intervening linkages of terrain that ensured the illusion of depth. In his painting now, this old and revered strategy was forsaken by a bold and dramatic choice. Simply due to the angle of viewing, the mountain appeared to thrust forward, the actual spatial depth between the mountain and the quarry all but eliminated. It was even possible to imagine the mountain advancing so far forward that the greenery along the top of the ravine edge appeared like a cushion upon which the great hulk of rock rested!

In the present state of his painting—as he had left it at the end of his last session here—the warm color qualities of the quarry rock were repeated in fainter tones through the mountain above, and this helped pull together the two masses even more. But as he looked at his work on this morning, Cézanne wondered if he had gone too far. Perhaps he should restore some distance between the foreground cliffs and the mountain behind. While the issue centered upon the way the masses of mountain and cliffs acted upon each other in space, there was always this latitude in choice of emphasis. How close or how far apart was a matter of feeling that he still had not resolved. From session to session his response to the site could change. It was all a matter of evolving feeling and process.

Today a blueness in the air threw the orange-colored quarry cliffs further forward than before. The color came off the quarry rock with force, the rusty reds, burnt oranges, and pale gray-yellows appearing most pronounced. He wondered how he would ever resolve it.

Then something new and unexpected began intruding into his meditations. More than usual, his attention on this morning was drawn to the vertical gap between the foreground cliffs. The opening was narrow at the top and gradually widened in sloping curves as it descended. The slender trunk of a pine tree, tilting to the left, was visible in the gap, with brush and grasses beyond. The greenery seemed to spill down from above, the gap appearing to him as a kind of natural funnel with vegetation pouring down. The idea, metaphorical of course, nevertheless seemed to have an optical reality for him as he studied the gap more closely. Even the rocky edges around the top of the opening tipped downward, reinforcing the sense of the funnel-like aperture. It was as if the brush on the top of the cliffs could slide toward this opening.

He studied the gap carefully, his eyes rising and descending slowly through the whole of its length. He raised his eyes straight up into the mass of the mountain. There he suddenly sensed the mountain itself hovering above the opening, as if in some way connected to it. Yes! The mountain itself, as its axis leaned slightly to the right, showed a tendency to tip toward the gap!

Cézanne drew back from his easel. Everything he had originally planned was becoming altered. Now he felt he was going too quickly and too far; his sensibilities were suddenly driving his imagination in a new direction for which he was unprepared at the moment.

He tried to focus on the motif as first conceived: the face of the ravine separated into two parts with the mountain above and the intervening space separating them more or less eliminated. In the original conception, the gap between the foreground cliffs was an interesting and even central element but not in this new way, not as such an active and driving force within the whole image.

Cézanne returned to his easel and looked again at the living landscape, comparing it with his painted image. He was uneasy in these new thoughts and decided to put them aside for the time being. He tried to turn to other problems. He reworked the tonalities of the rock quarry, intensifying the red and yellow hues and at the same time inserting some delicately shaded gray and blue tones into the mountain. Of course, the color changes he wrought upon the quarry rocks required corresponding changes in the greens of pine trees in the foreground. It was always this way: the alteration of one thing required an adjustment of something else. As he well knew, it would not take much modification in one part of the painting to call for big revisions elsewhere.

He painted steadily but without enthusiasm, working on those parts of the cliffs most removed from the gap. He knew that this latest idea about his motif, if he accepted it, meant a complete rethinking of the whole painting. When would it ever end, if at every turn something new arose? It more and more appeared to him as if the world and his viewing of it were locked in a perpetually evolving relationship, nothing fixed or stable, everything subject to change. He began to feel very irritated and restless.

He had been painting for more than an hour before he stopped again. He walked away from the painting, following the edge of the ravine for ten or fifteen paces. He was not pleased with where things stood. As much as he tried, he could not shake the new thoughts about the opening between the cliffs. These ideas bothered him as much as they excited him. The sensations he felt toward nature were complicated. The visible world in all its vast detail was always there for him to behold, but taking it in was not a simple or instantaneous process.

From where he stood, he looked back at the gap. The opening between the rocks now appeared severely narrowed due to the oblique angle from which he was viewing it. He moved slowly back along the edge of the ravine toward his easel, watching the gap widen as he approached it. Once opposite the opening, he again became engrossed in the way the space between the two cliffs opened, leading the eye up into the mountain. Why had he not seen it in this way from the very first, so obvious and compelling was it now? As had happened many times before, he realized again how seeing is a sequential process and that the mind takes in what it will only through time.

His mind, almost against his will, continued to think playfully about the gap in the rock wall and how it might relate to the mountain above it. He noted how the one was directly over the other, the gap rising straight up into the heart of the vast mass above it.

Suddenly his imagination made another leap: the gap marked where the mountain was most firmly rooted to the earth from which it rose. The gap signaled the place where the mountain and the earth were locked together.

Then in a final act of recognition, he envisioned a way of expressing this relationship in his painting. The possibility grew directly out of what he was now seeing for the first time. The left side of the Mount Sainte-Victoire rose diagonally more or less in a straight, unbroken contour, while the right side was far more uneven; it bent and curved in three major places. In effect, there was a kind of buckling of the right-hand contour on the side of the peak most directly over the gap in the cliffs below. It appeared to him that the mountain itself, in a strange way, was bending toward the gap!

Could he not simplify the contours of the mountain in such a way that would make this relationship more apparent, the near and the far locked into a kind of dance, each acknowledging the other? Yes!

Now he knew he had to stop. His mind was running away from him. He put down his brushes and sat for a few moments on the trunk of a fallen pine tree. The daring of his ideas both excited and frightened him. Could he really get away with this? Could he make such a relationship plausible within the framework of his painting? He would need to let all this settle down in him. He decided that he should pack up and go back to the abandoned stone cabin where he rested sometimes when he worked here in the quarry. He had brought something to eat, and he could ponder all that had just occurred.

He set about packing up his things and then turned one more time to face the mountain and the wall of the ravine. The sight thrilled him and then, as he slowly walked away, he fell to worrying about these new meanings of the opening in the ravine wall. He wondered if he could find a way to express his new ideas with the paint itself, not just through the colors and the tones but by the very manner in which the brushstrokes were laid down. What if the strokes themselves bent toward the opening? Yes!

5

GIVERNY

CLAUDE MONET threw his head back and laughed. "I hear he thinks I'm only an eye!"

"Yes, but 'what an eye!' Don't forget that part," replied Pierre Renoir excitedly. "He says that too. I think he really means it as a compliment, Claude."

Both men laughed.

Monet raised the wine bottle to refill his friend's glass. The two painters sat in a sun-filled room in Monet's comfortable country house in Giverny, surrounded by a large garden richly planted with trees and flowers and a pond filled with water lilies.

"Actually, Claude, you came off fairly well in his judgment. He thinks my paintings look too cottony and that poor Pissarro's art peaked twenty years ago and hasn't been as good since. How do you like that?"

Monet, half-smiling, shook his head and said, "Poor Paul. He's furious with us again."

"Apparently," said Renoir. "He told Émile Bernard that compared to himself we are all asses. Nobody can paint a red like him, he says."

"Ah, the poor bedeviled fellow," complained Monet. "He even takes down his friends."

"Oh, don't worry about that too much," replied Renoir. "You know him as well as I do. His opinions about us all gyrate like a top: he loves us, he hates us. And at the center of all that spinning, his own opinion of himself goes round and round, too. Tomorrow he will have forgiven us for whatever he thinks we've done...or not done. He'll be singing our praises because he'll be down on himself again. Has there ever been a painter harder on himself?"

"And now he's suddenly coming right out into the open," responded Monet, searching in his pockets for his cigarettes. "Vollard's got his show scheduled for sometime late this year. Imagine, now over a hundred paintings at once, I've heard, when before this, there's only been a trickle ever seen at one time. To have talked him into it, Vollard must have had a silver tongue."

Monet located his Caporals Roses, drew one from the pack, and lit it.

"I've heard he's sending Vollard 150 paintings, Claude, but you sound skeptical. Don't you approve? This is a big opportunity for Paul—a chance to turn a few heads and prove a thing or two."

Renoir spoke with great earnestness, not believing his friend could really have a serious objection to this unexpected opportunity for their difficult but respected colleague.

To add a further note of urgency, Renoir declared, "Do you realize he's never had a solo show? Never in his life. Anywhere!"

"Oh, of course I support him," Monet said. "What do we go through all this for if not to exhibit the results of our little studies...our little experiments in colored pigment, eh? And sell all we can, by God!" he added with a laugh, as he gestured toward one of his canvases hanging on a wall near him.

"But I'm just thinking of him," he went on. "He's so vulnerable. The practical affairs of life are so beyond him. For a few of us...sure...his show is going to be wonderful. To see a body of his work? I'll love it. But you know about the rest of them. If the art crowds pay any attention at all...if they even bother to go by Vollard's gallery...they'll eat him alive. They'll hoot and scream and beat the walls with their fists. 'That's not painting!' they'll shout. 'Any donkey can do that!' they'll sneer. That's what I worry about. What is he letting himself in for? And he must worry about that, too."

With a sigh Renoir slowly nodded his head in agreement. "You're right. They won't understand. They'll be as brutal and ignorant as always. And as blind. But what choice does he have? What choice did any of us have?"

"None...absolutely none," said Monet. "But I'm just curious about why now...after all these years of isolation. It seemed to me he'd pulled back...protected himself...kept out of the way. Oh, I know he's sent work to the Salon, but that seemed as much a gesture of defiance as anything else. Had they accepted one of his paintings, he would have been as surprised as anyone. I can't recall when I saw him last. How about you?"

Renoir shrugged and held up both hands in a gesture expressing that he couldn't remember either.

"He's always had a flair for the dramatic, hasn't he?" said Renoir, smiling. "Remember the times he used to suddenly appear at the Café Guerbois? The way he'd sit there with us for a while without speaking. Not a single word...not a greeting to anyone...nothing. And then he'd just as suddenly get up and leave. And those outlandish clothes he wore! I always thought he did that just to irk Degas and Manet, who were always dressed to the nines. Remember? He used to drive them crazy. Were you there the time Manet tried to shake his hand and Paul pulled back, saying, 'Ah, Monsieur Manet, I cannot shake your hand. I have not bathed for a month.' And don't forget his favorite saying, 'You'll never get your hooks into me.'"

"No, Pierre," Monet corrected. " His favorite saying was, 'Life, how frightening it is.'"

Both men laughed.

"No, we must stop. This is cruel," said Renoir. "We mustn't laugh. For him none of this is a joking matter. When he says those things, he's serious. He means them. Life really does terrify him."

"I know you're right, Pierre, but you must admit, he's a character of such extremes. It reminds me of the first time he met Mary Cassatt. It was right here, you know; I introduced them. Did she ever tell you?"

"No, I don't believe so."

"It was a rare visit here for Paul. He was actually in the area for about a week. He stayed at the inn at Vernon and came to me two or three times. He was here at my fifty-fourth birthday party. That's when he met Rodin and Clemenceau. Weren't you here too?"

Before Renoir could even answer, Monet plunged ahead with his story.

"Anyway, Mary came a couple of days later. She really didn't look forward to meeting him. She'd heard all the rumors and the gossip…his gruffness and so forth. And at first sight it all seemed true. His dress, his abruptness. The fierce looks he can make when he's nervous or upset. It was only later at the table that she saw another Paul. As the evening progressed, she came to realize how wrong she had been. Under the rough looks and manners, he was extraordinarily courteous and deferential, even if he ate with his knife, scraped the soup bowl with his spoon, and drank off the remainder right out of the bowl!"

Renoir laughed.

"And she said Paul always prefaced his opinions with, 'For me...' or, 'In my opinion...' never forcing his ideas on anyone else. 'The most liberal artist I've ever met,' she said. How do you like that, Pierre?"

Renoir, recollecting something else, asked, "Did you ever read that short piece Duranty wrote about a crazy, fantastical artist he called Maillobert? A mad bit of writing. It was in that book that came out right after he died, back in '80 or '81. Maillobert was hidden away in his dark and dingy den of a studio, the walls packed with enormous paintings...hideous figures leering out through piles of thick, dirty paint that by turns had been scrubbed and troweled onto the canvas. Total chaos. Oh, it was wild...obscene, even. The portrait of the artist gone mad. I'm trying to remember who told me that our dear old Paul was the inspiration for this crazy Maillobert!"

"But doesn't that make my point, Pierre? That's exactly the artist whose work they'll all go to Vollard's to see. And believe me, that's who they will see! Their minds will be made up ahead of time. That mad person is the only one they'll permit themselves to see."

"Duranty should have known better," said Renoir. "He was our friend, our supporter. He was our spokesman on more than one occasion."

"Yet even he," said Monet, "fell into the trap. Paul simply breeds misunderstanding and scorn."

Monet started shifting around in his chair. He was getting

worked up about the risks, as he saw it, to which his friend was exposing himself. He went on.

"His movements and his whereabouts are so obscure and his work almost invisible. He's the perfect stuff to make rumors out of, and that is just what has happened. Since so few people know him, people like Duranty have invented him. The image of Paul and his art is so overblown and distorted that in some people's minds he's become a kind of wild man roaming the countryside around Aix and Paris. It's ridiculous. Next they'll be sending the police to arrest him!"

Monet stamped out his cigarette, got up from his chair, and walked to the window, where he stood with his hands joined behind his back. He stared out into his garden. Then, turning back to his friend, he said, "Now when he suddenly comes forward with a large body of his work, I'm just afraid people will only see what they want to see. His paintings will confirm the worst instead of enlighten."

"You may be right," answered Renoir. "It's so depressing. And I've seen others hold the most distorted and uninformed views about him. George Moore, for one, who also should know better. Even a mind like Huysmans' was put off for a long time. Our writer friends struggle and err in their assessments. Yes, you're right, it's his absence and the rarity of his work in places where it can be seen that promotes most of the bizarre and distorted ideas about him and his work. And he never seems to raise a finger to quell any of the rumors. At least his work will be seen for a change. I wonder what Camille thinks about all this."

At the mention of Pissarro's name, Monet pulled a watch from his pocket and turned again toward the window. "Where is he? Camille's train should have arrived in Vernon half an hour ago. Sylvain went to pick him up. They're both probably dawdling on the road somewhere. I want to show both of you my London paintings after lunch."

As if in answer to his concern about the arrival of Pissarro, the cries of Lily, Monet's step-granddaughter, rose from the garden, her laughter penetrating the room where the two artists were so earnestly talking. Monet, who was still standing by the window, saw his old friend coming toward the house along the wide graveled path of the Grande Allée, the principal route through the gardens.

"Ah, there he is now, Pierre, and none too soon."

Monet opened the door to the front hall just in time to see Pissarro picking up Lily in his arms. He also saw Sylvain leading away the horse and cart. From another part of the house Monet's wife, Alice, approached. Renoir joined Monet in the doorway and waved. Monet moved forward to greet his old colleague and to inquire of Alice how much time remained before lunch would be served.

Once back in the house, Renoir and Monet took their places again in the room where they had been talking. Pissarro chose an empty chair beside Renoir and accepted the glass of wine Monet handed him.

"Your gardens look as enchanting as ever, Claude," Pissarro said. "Sylvain tells me you're enlarging the pond in the water garden. A new series of paintings on the way, I suspect."

"Perhaps," replied Monet. "If I can just get my London paintings behind me, then I'll see. Right now I'm floundering in my own painted Thames. By comparison, the water-lily pond is a puddle."

All three men laughed.

"Yes," said Pissarro, "I saw Durand-Ruel a couple of days ago. He talked to me about your London paintings. I think he wants to get his hands on them, and the sooner the better. Is he going to give you another exhibition?"

"Don't talk to me about him," replied Monet with a note of irritation in his voice. "He's driving me crazy. I've got about ninety canvases in progress in the studio, all of them of London. I can't even let one of them go right now, not until I get things further along. To work on any one of them I need all the others around me, and Durand-Ruel will just have to wait."

"Ninety paintings all at once!" cried Renoir.

"Yes," roared Monet, "you should have seen my rooms at the Savoy in London. I had paintings stacked everywhere. Half the time I couldn't find the ones I wanted when the light and fog effects outside my window reappeared."

"I'm trying to imagine what your bill must be just for all the stretchers and canvas!" laughed Renoir.

"Don't even ask."

"How differently we all approach our work, eh?" mused Pissarro. "Well, Claude, I certainly envy your situation and admire your nerve. Personally, right now I'd do just about anything to get Durand-Ruel to take more of my work, and here you are holding him off. He wants my older paintings but not my recent ones. As if an artist doesn't work through certain ideas to go on to other ideas. Durand-Ruel says that as far as he's concerned, an artist should just have one style, and only one! Can you imagine?"

"You mean your dot paintings?" interrupted Renoir with a smile and a wink in Monet's direction.

"No, he doesn't want those either," replied Pissarro, frowning. "You know that. Besides, I've completely abandoned pointillism...and you know that too."

"Yes, you came back to your senses at last, eh, Camille?"

continued Renoir, who would not let up his teasing. "Seurat really got hold of you for a while, didn't he?"

"Never mind," retorted Pissarro. "That young group has something important to say. You and the others will see. I'm proud to have worked with them as long as I did. It's just that I came to realize my temperament requires a less rigid approach…a more…"

"Less rigid? My God, Camille, you must have suffocated working inside that straitjacket of…"

"Come on, you two," laughed Monet. "All that's over now for Camille."

All three looked at each other and paused for a moment in silence. Then Pissarro spoke up, "Oh, all right then, how about this?"

The old painter picked up a slender briefcase he had brought that now lay beside his chair. He extracted a newspaper from it.

"I read this on the train this morning on the way out here. When I got to Vernon I was hot enough to pick a fight. If anyone connected with the Academy had been within shouting distance, he'd have gotten an earful!"

Monet and Renoir looked at Pissarro, alarmed by his uncharacteristic anger.

"What can it be?" asked Renoir. "You're usually so calm."

"Yes…yes, I know, Pierre, but things are not so good for me right now. My eye, for one thing. It continues to trouble me. And my work is just not selling. It's maddening. And then on top of all that, it's so infuriating to have to read these imbecilic opinions by such a pompous ass."

"Who is it this time?" asked Monet.

"Bouguereau again," replied Pissarro. "Another one of his asinine interviews."

"More pronouncements from Mt. Olympus?" sighed Renoir. "What now?"

"It's just one more proof," answered Pissarro, "of how little progress we have made over the years in converting people to our point of view."

Pausing, Pissarro scanned quickly down the article to the passage he wanted to read. He fixed the place with his finger and looked up at the others.

"I can't bear to read the whole thing again, but listen to this little bit. It'll give you an idea of his drift. 'Have you ever seen blue shadows? Do you think it is clever to create women who sweat rainbows? Yes! Women perspiring in prismatic colors...'"

Pissarro paused to glance up at his two friends as Bouguereau's words registered on their faces.

"Don't you love the images? Aren't they perfect? 'Sweating rainbows...prismatic colors...!' After more than twenty years that's all he thinks of our work. And the old bastard goes on, listen. 'There are color-blind people, but that's not my fault! There are others who think it is painting. What do you want me to do about it?' Now here's the best part. 'There is only one nature and only one way to see it.' How do you like that? Only one way to see it...his way, of course."

Pissarro flung the newspaper down on his lap.

"No blue shadows," cried Monet, laughing. "After all this time, we as a group have painted enough blue...and red and purple and cadmium orange to make all Paris sweat rainbows! At this point, I don't need Bouguereau, and you don't either."

Renoir, joining in with Monet's good spirits, added, "Yes, Camille, why get bothered now? What do you expect? That old fart has fought us from the very beginning. The man's mind is enclosed in stone."

"Yes, yes…I know, I know. But we should never take such talk lightly," pleaded Pissarro. "Don't you see? That's the same stuff they were saying twenty-five years ago. Think of it! We haven't gained a step in all that time."

"Ah, my friend," said Monet, "you take it too hard. You exaggerate. After all, we have our partisans. We have our friends."

"And our collectors," added Renoir, trying to alter Pissarro's sour mood.

Seeing that he was getting nowhere, Pissarro shook his head and fell silent.

Then Renoir, thinking suddenly of the conversation he and Monet had had earlier about Cézanne, said with a smile, "Paul's show at Monsieur Vollard's this year will spread around a few more square yards of prismatic colors, don't you think? I hope they drag old Bouguereau by just to make his flake-white beard turn scarlet with rage."

Monet and Renoir both laughed heartily and, watching them, Pissarro could not resist a smile.

"Just before you arrived, Camille, we were talking about our old and difficult friend," said Renoir. "Claude is concerned about the reception Paul's work will get and how he will deal with it. Of course, we all know that there will be plenty of hoots and hollers and a great deal of other commotion…"

"If they even notice," interjected Monet. "That, of course, is the other possibility, you see: that no one except a few friends will even go by to see the work."

"Oh, I wouldn't worry about that," said Pissarro, trying to shake off his bad mood brought on mainly by the newspaper article. "It's a huge step for Paul just having the show, whatever happens. Think of the years it's been. Actually, none of us, I suspect, has had a good long look at his work for a long, long time. It's mostly been a little something here…a little something there. Always very tantalizing…very provocative.

"The last time I really had a good look at what he was doing was when he used to come out and paint with me around Auvers and Pontoise. That was a long time ago now. In the early '70s we spent a lot of time together. We talked then a lot and shared everything we were tying to do. That's when I think I got him looking outside of himself at nature. He was like a piece of fruit ripe for picking. It was wonderful watching him open up to our ideas about color and light."

Pissarro shifted his body in his chair. He paused thoughtfully and then went on.

"Persuading Vollard to take him on when nobody else would…and then getting Paul to agree is already a triumph of sorts, don't you see? In my enthusiasm to get Vollard to do this, I even told him I'd let him show Paul's paintings from my collection. But I must say, as the time grows nearer, I'm starting to regret saying that. I realize I don't really want to part with any of them!"

"But how did Vollard talk Paul into an exhibition as big as this?" asked Renoir. "So many paintings. More works than Vollard's little gallery can hold, it seems to me."

"Well, " said Pissarro, "I don't mind saying, I guess I'm as responsible as anyone for getting Monsieur Vollard to approach Paul. I badgered him…I pleaded with him. He finally tried but only succeeded when we enlisted Paul's son, who represented the case with great earnestness to his father. You know Paul has this strange, inexplicable confidence in his son's worldliness. It's really a case of his own insecurity that lets him invest such trust in his son, who, to be frank, has never struck me as someone endowed with exceptional gifts of any kind."

"I know what you mean," said Renoir. "I've myself heard Paul speak with such fondness and admiration about his son's presumed understanding of the world, qualities that he feels are utterly lacking in himself. It's bewildering but quite touching, even if mostly unfounded. You know, Camille, of all of us who have been his friends over the years, you've probably been the most loyal to him for the longest time. You've always stood by him, defending his painting no matter what, even when some of the rest of us...what shall I say?...held back."

"Well, perhaps you're right," Pissarro acknowledged. "I've believed in his talent from the first. I still remember when Oller introduced me to him at the Académie Suisse back in the '60s. His drawings had a unique quality even then. And when we worked together in the '70s, I watched him blossom. But don't think I haven't been angry with him. We all know him. He's treated all of us badly at some time or other. Such sensibility and yet such a lack of balance. But I have other news about our friend's upcoming exhibition at Vollard's."

Pissarro paused as he put his thoughts in order.

"Émile Bernard came to me three days ago with a request from some young friends of his. When Paul's work is being exhibited, they would like to honor him with a small banquet. And they would like to do it as a surprise—to get him somewhere under some pretext and then all show up to pay him homage. That's where I think we come in. Most of these young people are aspiring artists themselves and have seen Paul's work at Tanguy's over the years. They have evidently joined in a little group that has its base in the fierce loyalty they feel for him. You must admit it's touching. Bernard assures me that their sincerity is genuine; he also said their means are modest. Bernard, who spent that time with him in Aix for that month a while back, could invite Paul easily enough. But he wonders if one of us—his older friends—would be more apt to persuade him to participate. And Émile wonders, Claude, if you would be willing to host the evening here. What do you think?"

Before Monet could answer, Renoir spoke up.

"What a capital idea! What fun and what pleasure it should give Paul after all these years. I'll be happy to write to Paul...or you do it yourself, Camille."

Pissarro looked at Monet, who had a pensive, doubtful expression on his face.

"It's a nice idea, but it'll never work."

"Why?" asked Renoir in surprise.

"Because he'll never come."

"Dammit, Claude, how do you know that?" cried Renoir in exasperation. "Surely..."

"Don't you remember when we tried to do this before?" interrupted Monet. "It was right here then, too. You were with us, weren't you, Pierre? Paul simply got up and ran off. We'd only raised a toast to him, and he walked right out on us without a word. He was absolutely unable to trust our sincerity. He left the next morning without even saying goodbye to me. I had to send his things back to Aix. He thought we were making fun of him."

Renoir and Pissarro looked at each other, both nodding their heads in agreement as they recalled the incident. They knew that their friend's dour assessment was probably right. It was quite possible that their colleague from Aix would not appear at any party, even one celebrating him, as touchy and insecure as he was.

"And I'll make one more prediction: Paul won't even come to Paris to see his own show!"

"Now you've gone too far, Claude," said Renoir. "Surely he'll come to see his own work. He must!"

"Why must he?" retorted Monet. "If I were him I'd think twice about it. The dangers are bad enough if you have the skin of an ox. For someone as fragile as he is, the risks are frightening."

Pissarro leaned back in his chair, taking in this exchange, and then finally spoke. "Well, my friends, let's not run too far ahead of the facts. Claude may be right, but we should let Paul decide himself. I suggest we go ahead with Bernard's request. If you both agree, I'll write to Paul. If need be, one of you can write a follow-up invitation later."

"Yes," said Renoir. "I like that. However unlikely our prospects, we should try."

"And if he consents," added Monet, "we can, of course, hold the affair here. It would be a pleasure for Alice and me."

Just as Monet finished speaking, the three men heard a faint knocking from across the room. Slowly the door opened and then, down low, the little face of Lily came into view.

"Lunch is ready, Grandpa," said the small voice.

"There's my Lily!" cried Monet, beckoning to her with open arms. Stepping hesitantly into the room, the little girl looked shyly at Renoir and Pissarro and then with a shout of laughter ran to her stepgrandfather, who pulled her onto his lap as she hid her face in his arms. Still holding Lily, Monet rose to his feet.

"To table, my friends. In honor of our difficult colleague, we have some of Madame Cézanne's ragout of cod awaiting us!"

6

Cézanne's Dream

IN THE LAST MOMENTS OF DAYLIGHT, Cézanne arrives exhausted at the doorstep of his house in town. The walk down the hill from his studio on this cold, windswept day seems longer and more tiring than usual. His head aches and a deep fatigue fills his body. Although he has striven with great effort to advance his painting, he has achieved nothing of significance. At one point, he became so angry he nearly destroyed the canvas on which he had been working for more than a week. He checked his frustration by furiously scraping away most of what he had painted this day.

Finally at his doorway, his hand shakes as he fumbles with the key in the latch. Once inside, he barely has the strength to take off his hat and heavy coat and climb the stairs to his bedroom. There is no question of trying to eat anything. In a feverish state, he throws himself, fully clothed, on his bed. He only means to lie there for a few moments to recover the energy to undress himself but immediately falls into a deep, dream-filled sleep...

...The light pushes back the dark...The objects before him are pulled toward the light...Even the window and the door...dominated

*by the light...bend toward it...He fixes his eyes on the space between
the apple and the gray-green jar...The apple to one side...The jar to the
other...And between them...only a few square inches...the space that
separates the two objects...The space that to him is as real as the objects
themselves...As if his task is to paint that space...not just the two
objects surrounding the space...though these too of course...but especially the space between them...the space itself...If he could just paint
the objects and have the space between them be there too...But he's tried
that many times...in many ways...It is never that simple...It is never
that direct or easy...There is something else...some ineffable quality
about the space that he can never quite catch...but which is essential...
The space itself has its own properties...Of an entirely different nature
than the objects of course...but real in its own way...Space...after
all...is a thing too...Space surrounds and engulfs the objects in it...It
contains them...It contains everything...Space is a giant vessel that
contains everything...It provides the setting in which the world around
him unfolds...It is the means by which all things are distinct from one
another...by which they have their own place...where they can breathe
and be themselves...Space is the means by which all things face each
other...Space is the backdrop against which all things become visible...
Finding a way to express these qualities of space is his chief problem...
But how to make this space he sees and feels...to be visible in his painted
version of it?...He calmly sits in front of the still life before him...
brushes and palette in hand...The colors are laid out in the usual
order...The canvas is ready to receive the summations of his observations and judgments...It surprises him how relaxed he feels...That is
not to say that he is not puzzled...even perplexed...As so often before...
he is quite awed by his task...But this time he is close...He is almost
getting it...He senses it there...the space...He feels its presence...A
sense of the air in the space and the light in the air...The light and the
air occupying the space...The all-pervading light wanting to fill the*

space...Rushing through it in all directions at once...The light glancing off the plane surfaces of the objects in its path...Touching them... Striking them...Grazing against them in its headlong flight...Caressing them...Making all things it brushes against to light up...To become visible...But recklessly hurtling on...Deflecting...Bouncing... Careening...Never stopping...The light forever trying to get beyond whatever interrupts its outward rush...As if all objects are obstacles to be hurtled past...The light to go on forever in space...Trying always... desperately...to be at one with space...To fill...even to the last corner... all of space...Ever outward from its source...As if the light would go as far as the space would go...Such a fruitless...impossible...ambition... to fill the immensity of space...But such is the folly of the light... whether of suns or candles...He pauses...He compares the real space between his objects with his representation of it in his painting...No!... It is not right...Once again the space in the painting is not right...The mysterious and indispensable quality has slipped away again...As if it is something he can see...he can feel...but which he cannot touch...It is maddening...It is so discouraging...He sees it...he feels it...but he cannot capture its image...its essence...He pulls back...He tries to find the point where he has gone wrong...For a moment...he is overcome with hopelessness...He drops his arms...The one hand almost lets go of his brushes...His body sags...Minutes pass...Finally he turns back to face the still life again...the apple and the gray-green jar...His emotions calm down somewhat...His head clears somewhat...He pulls himself together and tries again...He must go back to the beginning... He must rethink everything...As he stares at the little space between his objects...he realizes once again that its visibility seems to depend upon the objects that surround it...The boundaries of the space are right beside the boundaries of the objects...The space he sees...in the most elementary...common sense terms...is the simple outcome of the objects that surround it...The space is what is left over...The space is what is *there where the objects are not...The space is the presence of the absence of the objects!...But this ancient idea of space as mere emptiness does not fit the facts...At least not his facts...Not the facts as he sees them... As he experiences them...That is his problem...always...his experience of the facts...He looks hard again at the situation before him...He notices that the space fits exactly between the two objects...The space fits exactly in between the two objects...He reaches out and moves the apple...He pushes it closer to the jar...The space that separates the two objects shrinks...Then he pushes the apple away...The space expands... The size and mass of the apple do not change when he moves it...but the size of the space does...The space between the apple and the jar opens and closes dramatically...He does this several times...The space always changes according to where he positions the apple...This is something he has done many times in the course of preparing his still lifes...getting the spaces to work...What he sometimes thinks of as the "intervals" between things...is a problem over which he always spends a lot of time...One could even say that he agonizes over this point... The fluid quality of space...Its ability to contract and expand according to the way objects impinge upon it...This is something that utterly fascinates him...Suddenly...with an almost impulsive gesture...he reaches out and snatches up the apple!...Then...when he concentrates again on the edge of the space that just an instant before fitted so perfectly up against the contour of the apple...he finds it is gone!...That whole side of the space pressing so tightly up against the apple has collapsed...disappeared...like a wave gone back into the sea...What had been there the moment before...so clear and definite...was now dissipated into the larger...undifferentiated space created by the absence of the apple...He stares for some time at what is now...without the apple there...the undefined space that just a moment before had a clear shape as it nestled up against the apple...Then...just as suddenly as before... when he took it away...he returns the apple to its place next to the jar...*

The entire side of the space that had disappeared...that had collapsed... instantly reappears...completely restored...Amazing!...These transformations are part of the mystery of space that intrigues him so...A sudden wave of discouragement comes over him again...Feeling a need to escape his dilemma...he turns his gaze away from the space between the apple and the jar...He seeks out the larger horizon surrounding him...Carefully raising his eyes...he directs them to the other side of the room...Up the table leg with slow steady gaze...Across the tabletop...inch by inch...Slowly along the contours of each object standing there...The side of the glass bottle...Around the curve of the vase... Along the edge of each piece of drapery...Then he moves his eyes along the sides of the canvases stacked up against the wall...Next he makes his eyes move onto the place in the corner of his studio where he hangs his hat and his coat...He peruses each fold carefully in sequence... slowly...both eyes in unison...Coming full circle...finally his eyes come to rest among the many brushes...the tubes of paint...the palette...the jars of oil and solvents and the rags that are on the table beside him... He looks at the clusters of brushes crowded into the cans and jars in which he keeps them...There are dozens of long slender handles and various bristles stiffly sticking up...like flowers in a cramped bouquet... Some of them are scraggly and worn...Others are fuller...straighter... delicately tapered...He looks between the brushes at the space...It is everywhere...It surrounds everything...He glances down among the heap of paint tubes and the cans of oils and varnish...There is space everywhere...It is even in the folds of his smeared and stained paint rags...Space is in between the tiniest openings...It is inside the narrowest cracks and slits...He reaches out and moves some of the brushes... The space immediately alters...Some of it disappears...Space is like some verminous creature that infests everything...Space clings to everything...It surrounds everything...He looks down at his hands lying in his lap...Space is there too...It is between the hands...the fingers...He wiggles his fingers...The space between them adapts and reforms to every movement...effortlessly...He holds both hands in front of himself...palm facing palm...the fingers very straight...There lies the space between them...He sees it clearly...It fits exactly...conforming to the precise shape of his hands...He slowly moves his hands apart...In perfect unison space fills in every part...It fills in along every contour and surface as he further draws his hands apart...Then he closes his hands rapidly...with a clap...The space collapses in perfect timing with the speed with which he brings his hands together...Wonderful!... He had drawn the obvious conclusions long before now...Space...in order to be visible...has an undeniable dependency on things...It cannot exist...or at least it cannot be seen...except in the presence of things...Things need to be present in order to give space a shape... Things need to be present in order to provide it with the boundaries that are necessary for it to have a form...Without things...space is formless to the eye...It is invisible...It is infinite...He returns his gaze to the apple and the jar...He stares at the space between them...What is he to do?...The contours of the apple and the jar are perfectly contiguous with the edges of the space...For all practical purposes...they are identical...Or are they?...Perhaps that is precisely the point...Is the sea the land's edge also?...He fixes his eyes on a place along the contour of the apple...He stares unblinkingly for a full minute...Then...lifting his eyes from the apple...he moves them with slow and careful deliberateness...to a place along the edge of the jar...He stares again...Something does not seem right...He returns his eyes to a point on the edge of the apple...Then back to the jar...Then to the apple again...Suddenly he understands...When he focuses on a point along the contour of the apple...the jar blurs out...It does so just a tiny bit...He cannot see it with the same clarity as he now sees the apple...Then when he moves his gaze to a point on the edge of the jar...the apple becomes less distinct...Again...by only a tiny bit out of focus...but sufficient to be noticeable...He tests this several times...Then he tests it several more times...He pulls back...He turns his head...He rubs his eyes...and tries again...First the apple...Then the jar...Whichever contour he chooses to look at...he sees it clearly...At least he sees that part of it upon which his eyes focus...for even the upper and lower reaches of the contour of the jar blur out unless he moves his eyes up and down the edge...But the point here is that he can only see...one contour...or part of it...at a time...He cannot hold both contours...the apple's and the jar's...in the same focus at once...although they are only a few inches apart...To see them both in focus...he needs to move his eyes from one to the other...In order to take them both in...he has to glance back and forth...To do otherwise always leaves one of them slightly out of focus...His visual field...has its sharpest focus at the center...only there...It's just a tiny area of perfect focus in his field of vision... Then...as objects situate themselves farther and farther from that central focus...they gradually decline in clarity...They do this until...on the hazy periphery of his vision...the appearance of things becomes so insubstantial...that it dissolves into formless perturbations of light... By just moving his eyes...his whole field of vision...all the objects in it...shift...Some of them come plainly into view...Others recede...Still others all but disappear...It is as if before him...there extends a visual plane...or horizon...that reconstitutes itself at every movement of his eyes...Each object...or part of an object...picked out by his eyes from among the array of things packed into his field of vision...causes everything else to become its background...To see one thing perfectly... actually only a tiny part of one thing...he surrenders everything else to some degree of lesser clarity...Behind the thing seen...always...lies a horizon of continually shifting and unfolding things...At each movement of his eyes...the field is perpetually reforming and reconstituting everything within it...At each movement of his eyes...sometimes it seems to him...that the horizon...is not so much an element external to *himself...but something within him...As if it is a function of the level...and direction...of his own eyes...of his own body in relation to things...Yes!...*

Sudden, gruff cries from the street of a drunken man talking angrily to himself rouse the painter from his deep sleep but without fully waking him. He rolls over on his bed and in another moment slips back into an altered dream...

...Again the studio...Again seated at the table...brushes in hand...looking straight ahead...He seeks the objects he knows should be there...He looks for the space between the things...but finds them missing...Everything missing...The table empty...Where are his objects...his precious objects?...Dissolved into the space?...The space covering them?...Has the space become opaque?...Have the objects become transparent?...Anxiety begins to engulf him...Then something else occurs...A disturbance comes upon him for which he is quite unprepared...He hears a door opening...footsteps...voices murmuring... There is muffled talking in undertones...All of this is arising from one of the rooms beneath his studio...A shrill...derisive laugh...rises through the floor...It sweeps around his head...It bores right past his concentration inward...to throw his mind into frenzied alertness outward...He moans...He stiffens in his chair...In a voice half petrified with fright...he shouts..."Who's there?"...For an answer...only more laughter...more talk he cannot understand...and still more laughter... They do not hear him...Or if they do they pay him no heed...Why don't they hear him?...Or if they do...why don't they answer?...This is his property...These people have entered...unasked...into the rooms beneath his studio...No one...not anyone...has ever done that before!...

Every part of his mind is turned toward this intrusion…His project at hand…the still life…the missing objects…are…for the moment… forgotten…Instead…he directs his mind…with all his might…toward this frightening disturbance…He thinks of rushing downstairs to confront these intruders…He makes as if to move…Setting his arms…he leans forward and tenses his legs in preparation to raise his body from his chair…But instantly a great fatigue sweeps over him…He feels incredibly heavy…leaden even…He cannot get up…He tries again but it is no use…He weakly presses his body against the back of the chair… Rage…frustration…helplessness…all these feelings at once course through him…He goes limp…His body sags…His head falls forward… He sits there unable to move or think…the muffled noises from below adding to his confusion and his exhaustion…Minutes pass…Then as his concentration begins to reconstruct itself…he slowly focuses on the voices again…He strains to understand them…Their sounds rise and fall…but he cannot understand them…The words slur together…The words are muffled by what they must penetrate on their way to him… There is the ceiling in the room below…There are the thick boards of the floor in his studio…These together must create the barrier… Even when the voices grow louder…as they do from time to time… as if these intruders forget to whisper…still they are not clear…How they talk!…Sometimes they seem to be arguing…but about what?… He tries to separate out the intruders' voices…to try to understand how many there are…One voice is deep and gruff…His laugh is rude and vulgar…Another voice is high pitched and excitable…That voice seems always to question…or else to protest…If only he could understand them…He decides there are three intruders downstairs in the room below his studio…He decides that they are all male voices…The third voice is an infrequent one…But who are they?…Is one of them his gardener?…How dare Vallier bring men like this into his studio!…But none of them sounds like Vallier…But if not him…then who else?…

Solari?...Gasquet?...No...He doesn't think it is them either...So few people ever come around to his studio...No one ever comes to his studio!...Sometimes the voices trail off...Sometimes there is just silence... Or there is just someone laughing softly...giggling...Or sometimes someone speaks a sentence or two in a questioning voice...But no one answers...And one of them is always moving around...He hears constant footsteps moving back and forth...Once he thinks he hears..."Put it over there"...but that is only a guess...Oh, what are they doing?... They are looking at something...The thought comes upon him with frightening suddenness...MY PAINTINGS!...My God, they are down there looking at my paintings!...He tries to think of all the paintings he has stored down there...There are dozens of them...hundreds!... He has all kinds of works stacked down there...There are works of all sorts...in many states...Many are unfinished...Some are barely begun...There are none...of course...that are completely finished...He rarely does what he considers a finished painting...But no matter...this is no time to think about that!...There is the laughter again...This time it is particularly loud...He hears all three of them laughing at once... He knows it now...They are down there laughing at his paintings... He is enraged...He is frightened...He is embarrassed by these people downstairs who are laughing at his paintings...He feels exposed...He feels violated...Suddenly...one word emerges from among the raucous sounds below him......It is a word he hears distinctly...It somehow floats up...It somehow survives the passage through the ceiling and the floor...Until this moment...all the other words from below had been blurred by the ceiling and the floor...but this one word survives... This one word...after getting through the plaster of the ceiling and the thick boards of the floor...manages to hold itself together...It manages to keep its shape...It reaches his ears in a form he cannot mistake... Not only can he hear the word...he can understand it with ease and certainty...The word is a name...The word is a proper name...It is a

name that takes him so unawares that he sits frozen in place...unable
to move...One of the voices...the high nervous one...distinctly says...
FRENHOFER!...He stares straight ahead...With deadened eyes...
he forms the frightening name with pale lips soundlessly...He thinks
to himself..."They are looking at my paintings as they talk about
Frenhofer...They are comparing me to him...Oh...They are looking
at my paintings...and think I have failed like him..." He is beside himself...This is a terrible confirmation...He...of course...has thought of
that failed genius many times...He knows Balzac's story by heart...He
has known it for years...He has wondered many times...even out loud
when he was by himself...if he is not like Frenhofer...He has wondered
if he IS Frenhofer!...After all...is he not himself impotent before his
own vision?...Is he not himself unable to paint fully what he sees and
feels?...Is he not unable...truly...to realize his sensations?...But until
this moment...that was all his own musing...It was his own private
torment...But this is different...This is a matter of others reaching the
same conclusions...This is a matter of strangers...outsiders...looking at
his work in the rooms beneath his studio...and thinking these things...
The third voice...for the first time...speaks at length...It speaks in long
sentences...with fervor...with laughter...The third voice carries on for
some time...with some lengthy critique...But he cannot understand
the third voice any better than the other two...There is...however...a
quality in this third voice that strikes him differently...It is as if there
is something he recognizes...What is it?...He thinks it is something
about its intonations...something about its rhythms...Dammit...so
who is it?...He should know but he cannot get it...He cannot...Then
the gruff voice comes in again...There is more laughter...There is more
raucous...vulgar...laughter...Then the nervous one speaks...Then the
gruff one again...There is more moving about...There are noises...as
if lifting...Then the third voice again...It speaks with vigor...It speaks
with emphasis...It drives home a point...It hones in on some final

judgment…At the end of its statement…it gives off a shrill laugh…
The third voice gives off a long…ungenerous…spiteful laugh…Where
has he heard it?…He knows that laugh…

Oh…No…Not him…Please not him…My God, it's Zola!…

With sweat dripping from every pore, he wakes from his
dream to the sound of his own voice screaming, "Émile!"

7

The Second Visitation

Cézanne pushed open the wooden gate in the high wall that bordered the property where his studio stood. Passing through the opening, he carefully shut the gate behind him. No matter that on a given day the people who would pass by the little building on the hill would be few and thinly scattered. None, in any case, would ever think of disturbing his privacy.

Satisfied that the gate was properly latched, the old painter walked the few steps to the middle of the terrace where, standing by the linden tree that grew to one side, he looked out over the city of his birth. Spread out before him in the cool morning light, the city was at once a sight long since familiar and ever new. As many times as he had looked at every building, street, and tree there was to see from his terrace, the view defied total familiarization. There was an inexhaustible life of forms out there affected by the weather, the time of year, and the almost infinite number of ways his own perceptions sorted out the panorama. The power of space to shrink the size of objects turned the farther buildings into a kaleidoscope of tiny shapes. The clarity of the distant hills came and went depending upon the quality of the light and air. On this particular morning, the light was bright and the air exceedingly clear.

The single octagonal tower of the nearby cathedral of Saint-Sauveur loomed large above its surroundings, its stacked forms intruding vertically into the horizontal mass of the distant hills and mountains beyond. Cézanne, as he had done many times before, passed his gaze down through the curved and open stonework of the Gothic tower into the simpler geometries of the surrounding domestic architecture. He observed the changes of angles made by the planes of rooftops and walls as they spread out in all directions from the church structure. In the course of this recurring exploration he paused now and then to consider the visual impact of certain clusters of forms and contours, comparing their weight and density to what surrounded them or the transitions from one to the other, were he to make a painting of them at that moment.

The air at this early time of morning was invigorating, and Cézanne looked forward to an uninterrupted period of work on a new still life in his studio before the descent of the stifling heat. His appetite for painting aroused, he turned away from the urban scene before him and walked to the studio door, which he found ajar. This mildly surprised him; it was unusual that his gardener should have arrived this early. Without thinking more about it, he crossed the threshold and called out Vallier's name. The reply he got was as unwelcome as it was unexpected.

"Yo-ho, it's me," the cheery voice rang out. "Vallier is not here. Come up, come up."

Him! the old painter thought to himself. *Oh no, please not him!* It had been more than two months since his meeting with the stranger up among the steep rocks above the Château Noir. In the last few weeks, the worst of his memories of that encounter had begun to fade away. But the sound of this voice above him brought them all rushing back: the long list of accusations and insults, the almost psychic recall of things it did not seem this man could know, the irksome way the stranger found to lead him on and draw out things that Cézanne did not even want to think about, let alone discuss. And now this person had come back. For what? To pester him again? To take another day away from him? Another session of work sacrificed to this fellow's endless jabbering was more than he could stand.

"Dammit, no one except Vallier ever enters my studio when I'm not here!"

Scattered details of the dream he had had a few nights before came to mind. Fragmentary as his memory of it was, a fleeting recollection of unknown persons invading his space added uneasiness to his anger.

He began slowly to mount the stairs to his studio, but each step up raised his anger so that when he reached the upper floor he was more than ready to do battle. Charging into the middle of the large, light-filled room, fists clenched and jaw set, he bellowed, "How did you get in here?"

Looking wildly around, he saw no one.

"Over here behind the easel," said the chuckling voice.

The laughter spun the artist around, the sound drawing him straight to its source.

"There you are!"

In three strides he closed the distance between himself and his unwelcome visitor. The stranger was sitting jauntily with his legs crossed on a stool in front of the still-life painting the artist had planned to work on this morning. Much less formally dressed on this occasion, the outfit he wore nevertheless matched, garment for garment, clothes owned by the painter. Cézanne was too upset at the time to notice this detail, although he would recall it later.

"Marvelous morning, eh?" said the stranger, beaming. Pointing to the still-life painting, which was still in a very early state, he said, "I've been enjoying your new work here. I especially like the colors you are using. Some of the drawing, though, strikes me as odd. That jar, for instance. It's a little lopsided, don't you think?"

Seeing the artist's displeasure, the stranger quickly rephrased his comment. "No, not odd...I don't mean that at all. Let me say...unusual. Yes, the drawing of that jar is unusual."

"How did you get in here? Who let you in? You're trespassing on my property."

The exasperation in the artist's voice was clear. "Get out of my studio. I told you the last time I never wanted to see you again. No more talk. No more discussions. Leave my studio at once."

"You can be a little friendlier than that, can't you?" said the stranger. "I'm not a thief in the night come to steal your pictures. Really, old boy, you do me such injustice."

"'Old boy'?" Cézanne could not believe his ears.

"Oh no, not again," laughed the stranger. "We're not going to go through all this 'Who are you? I don't know you' business again, are we? You can't stand there now and say you don't know me. Not after our last meeting. To you, I should think, I'm rather unforgettable!"

The stranger turned a big smile on the artist but saw at once that his attempt at humor had fallen flat. Cézanne only glared and stood his ground. "Oh, what's the use?" said the stranger. "You can't imagine how disappointing this is. I told you before how much trouble I've gone to in order to be here. In the time since we met on that dreadful hillside at the Château Noir, I had hopes you would have thought this through differently. I know I said some hard things to you then, but I meant well. I had good intentions. I hoped you'd have seen that, but look what I find instead. You act as if I'm someone who comes to laugh at your work, to make fun of it."

The stranger paused, staring hard at the artist. "Are you afraid I'll compare you to Frenhofer?"

"What do you mean? Were you...?"

"No, no, forget I said that," interrupted the stranger. "I must confess I have the most perverse sense of humor. It does me no credit. None at all."

Again Cézanne was stunned by something the stranger seemed to know but yet could not know. The stranger tried to distract him.

"Those are paper flowers in your still life. Why don't you use real flowers?"

Cézanne pulled himself together and bellowed, "Enough! I don't want to hear another word. I just want you out of here. Now!"

Ignoring the artist, the stranger continued speaking. "You see, my great failing is that I'm such an optimist. I always think the best of people...expect the most from them in return. This is just the opposite of you. In fact *opposite* is the best possible way to describe you and me. I am outgoing and friendly; you are suspicious and withdrawn. I love people; you mistrust them. To me the absurd ways of the world are amusing; to you they are confusing and frightening. Where I step forward, you flee. To you, human relationships are baffling. To me, they are as transparent as glass."

The stranger had risen slowly to his feet. The two men faced each other barely a foot apart. White goatee faced white goatee, moustache faced moustache, bald pate shone unblinkingly at bald pate. They stared hard into each other's eyes. A slight movement of the stranger's lips suggested that he might speak again, but he remained silent. Instead, without turning his head or lowering his eyes, he reached behind himself to produce from somewhere a wide-brimmed hat, which he slapped down, slightly askew, onto his head. Even this unintentionally comic gesture did not penetrate the artist's stern looks.

"You're impossible," muttered the stranger, who squeezed himself between the easel and the unyielding artist. "It's too bad you won't let me stay long enough to tell you the news I have from Paris."

"What news?" asked the painter, faintly curious.

"Oh, it's about you…and what they are going to do."

"Who? What?"

"Oh, no, no…I'm sorry," jibed the stranger. "I can't tell you; there's no time now. You have made it perfectly clear that I must leave immediately."

"Who is going to do what?" repeated the artist, his curiosity suddenly on fire.

"I'm going now. You will never see me again. Goodbye."

"Damn you!" cried the painter. "You have this way of baiting me. But it won't work this time!"

In another step the stranger reached the head of the stairs and started to descend. The painter, watching, was caught in a moment of agonizing uncertainty as the striding figure started to disappear down the stairway.

"It was nice meeting you. I'll not bother you again," came the fading voice of the stranger, who was already partway down the stairs.

"Wait! Stop! Don't go!" said Cézanne as he rushed to the

head of the stairs.

The stranger, his back to the artist, paused in his descent. If the artist could have seen the look on the other's face he would have been suspicious all over again. The stranger had found the little edge he sought. Cézanne had snapped at the bait. Without moving and still with his back to the painter, the stranger took off his hat and spoke in a loud, firm voice. "What? You mean you don't want me to leave? You don't want me to get out of your life forever?"

Before Cézanne could answer, the stranger turned and started up the stairs again. "Yes, I do. I want you to leave." said the artist. "But tell me the news first, and then leave."

Without thinking, the artist stepped back and let the stranger pass him. In dismay Cézanne realized that he had lost his advantage. There the stranger stood in the middle of the studio, smiling at him.

"Wait a minute! What are you doing? Stop right there. What is this news of yours?"

"You have no idea how fortunate you are, dear fellow," the stranger said. "You have friends and admirers you don't even know. In a circle of young people in Paris you are celebrated, considered revolutionary, your painting is intensely discussed, you are defended with great energy in the cafes and the studios. Going to Tanguy's to see your paintings is a great event for them."

Cézanne looked flustered. All this praise and so-called support all of a sudden was something he was totally unused to. Abused and belittled for so long, he even had trouble accepting compliments from his few close friends and associates. True, lately there was the attention of one or two younger ones such as Émile Bernard and Louis Le Bail. And there was Gasquet's son, of course, with whom he had talked about his art. But it was too late for him now. Couldn't they understand that? He only wanted peace and quiet to continue his studies. He just wanted to be left alone.

Besides, thought the artist, *what is this all about? The first time we met, this awful man raved at me about how nobody cared, nobody understood my art. Now he's telling me there is this support from these young people. Apparently he will say anything, no matter how contradictory, if it gains him his end. But what is his end? I still don't know what he wants from me.*

"The prospect of your exhibition next month at Vollard's little gallery has caused a stir," the stranger went on. "Everyone who knows you is excited, of course, but some, like myself and Monet, are alarmed. Monet is very worried. He agrees with what I have tried to tell you: the public will reject you out of hand."

"Monet said that?"

"Perhaps not quite in those words, but that's what he meant. Of course he's pulling for you, but yes, he's very afraid. And I must warn you that they want to do something special for you, a celebration. They want to give a banquet in your honor."

"This is the news you have for me? This!"

"Why, yes. That's what…"

"No!" cried Cézanne. "I don't want them to do anything. Do you hear me? Nothing!"

"Of course you don't. This is why I'm telling you now, so you'll be ready for them. I know you don't want to go through that again. Remember the other time Monet had a party for you? They were all there to praise you. You were horrified. You became so suspicious and confused. Monet raised a toast in your honor, and you stormed out. Remember? You left them with their mouths hanging open. I know how you hate all that sort of thing. And now they want Monet to do it all over again."

The artist wondered how the stranger knew about that embarrassment at Monet's.

"Who is going after Monet with these ideas of honoring me? Who are they?"

"Well, it's these young people," the stranger told him. "It all started with them. They went to Émile Bernard to ask him to contact Monet and the others. You're not supposed to know about any of this; they want to surprise you. Renoir and Pissarro, I think, will probably be the ones to see to it that you are invited. Under some pretext or other, they'll get you out to Giverny..."

"Oh they will, will they? Well, I haven't even decided yet if I'm going to go to Paris at all. I just might stay here and not even go. What do you think of that?"

"Not even visit your own exhibition?" The stranger was flabbergasted. Such a possibility as that had never even crossed his mind. He paused, thought for a moment, and then rushed to seize his opportunity. "What a superb idea!" said the stranger excitedly. "Why, it's positively brilliant. They'll all be speechless. Not visiting your own show? This will be a sensation. A show like this is something that artists work toward for years, and for you to turn your back on it will be astounding. And, just think, you'll be spared all the outcries and all the praises too."

"A banquet?" said Cézanne. "Why should I go to hear them make up things they think they should say to me, things they think I want to hear? I don't need their praises. The more I think about it, the clearer it is to me that I should not go to Paris at all. I know their game. They just want to get their hooks into me. But I'm better than them all. I'm the best of them. Nobody can paint a red like me!"

The stranger grew very excited. Cézanne was responding to

the news about the banquet even more negatively than he had hoped.

"That's a stunning choice you have made. There are not many artists who could resist the temptation. But if you'll go that far, why don't you take the last logical step?"

"What?"

"Cancel the exhibition."

"Cancel the…?"

"Think of it! Wouldn't that show them all? None of them could get their hooks into you then. They'd all be stunned. They wouldn't know what to do, what to think. Your privacy would be kept intact. They wouldn't be pawing through your work. Meddling. Saying nasty things. You would be safe."

"But I've given my word to Monsieur Vollard. I can't just…"

"Yes you can. Of course you can. It's your work. You can do whatever you want. No one can tell you to do anything you don't want to do."

"But I must exhibit sometime."

"Dammit, Cézanne, you just don't get it, do you? You are such a bundle of contradictions. You scream and whine about not being understood. You hide out from everybody. You haven't exhibited for years. And now I'm telling you how to preserve your peace of mind, and you hesitate. You won't listen."

"But a painter must exhibit. I have sent frequently to the Salon."

"Don't make me laugh, Cézanne. Surely you are joking. What an exercise in futility that has been. You might as well hang your paintings on trees in the woods for the edification of squirrels and wild rabbits. They will look at your paintings with more sympathy and understanding than anyone at the Salon. As

I said last time, why expose yourself like this?"

"It's a question of readiness," Cézanne explained. "I have been persuaded that if a sufficient number of my paintings can be seen at one time together, my intentions will be better understood."

"So you actually think there is an audience out there? Poor man, you are more deluded than I thought. It's not even a question of a certain talent, you know. Even among those who can't stand your paintings, one or two admit to occasional passages of intriguing color in your pictures. As for ideas? You have plenty of those. Odd ones, to be sure. But it's your execution that is so hopelessly flawed. Your drawing especially."

The artist showed increasing anger in the expression on his face.

"Don't glare at me," said the stranger. "I'm just telling you what I hear. I keep my ears open, you know. I have access to many places. I know many people. Just follow my advice, and you won't regret…"

"Oh, shut up. I don't want to hear any more. Go away and leave me alone."

The stranger backed off. He sat silently for a moment looking at the artist, who turned his head toward the canvas he had been planning to work on.

"You are an amazing fellow, Cézanne. I marvel at your concentration and focus on the things of your work. When you are by yourself among your still-life objects or alone in the woods, you are one sort of person: open, alert, tenacious, aggressive. Of course, you struggle fiercely to express yourself through your art, and I know this never comes easily. You hold yourself to unimaginable standards beyond my comprehension. You are physically and emotionally drained by the effort and thrown from time to time into deep fits of depression. But somehow in those same periods you are whole and one with yourself and your surroundings. You raise the good fight; you go forward with firmness and determination. But let one human being enter your field of activity, and you are as helpless as a child. You are suspicious, mistrustful, ill at ease, frightened. It's as if the world of objects and the world of people are divided for you by a gulf that you cannot cross and remain the same person. You are so much more relaxed and at home with trees and rocks than you are with your fellow human beings. Alone and unwatched..."

"Dammit, stop analyzing me. I'm not a character in a book! What do you really know about me besides some stupid, trivial facts? As if facts ever explained anything. You don't know anything about how I feel or why I am the way I am."

The stranger could see that he was making little headway with Cézanne. In fact he might even be pushing him too far. He sought for a way to divert the artist from his rising anger.

After several minutes of strained silence, the stranger withdrew a slender book from his coat pocket. "I've brought you a little present. When I was in Paris last week I found this lovely edition of some of Baudelaire's poetry in a shop on Rue Vavin. The shop was just around the corner from where you lived in 1870, as a matter of fact. I thought of you immediately. I know how you love his poetry. I do too. Of course you have these poems in other books, but this copy has such a nice binding and lovely endpapers. Here, it's yours."

Cézanne glanced at the book but made no effort to take it. He turned back to his still life and began studying it. He looked back and forth between the still life itself and the painting of it he had begun.

The stranger watched carefully, not in the least offended by the artist's apparent rejection of the gift. As long as Cézanne got his mind off the subjects just now that were getting out of hand, that was all that mattered. Finally, the stranger ventured to speak. "I love Baudelaire's black period, don't you?"

The stranger waited patiently for Cézanne to react. The painter went on studying the objects before him.

"What black period?"

"Oh, you know, back in the early '40s when he always dressed in black. The black suits he wore no matter what the occasion or the season…or even the time of day. It was unheard of. For a time he was the talk of all Paris. For him black was the only color appropriate for an age in decline. As if he were in mourning for the period in which he lived. If that's what he thought then, what would he think if he were alive today, eh? Hah, can you imagine? It's been said that Baudelaire wore out his tailors with making black suits. But it only lasted a couple of years until he nearly went broke. It was during his terrible years of poverty afterward when I became interested in him."

"That's not what I want to hear about," said Cézanne suddenly.

"What? His dressing in black? Well, yes, I guess I can understand that. Elegance of dress is not part of your artistic vision, is it?"

The painter looked up sharply.

"No, no, forget I said that. I take that back. The way you dress is of no consequence. It has nothing to do with the business between us."

The painter was about to answer but turned back instead to his still life, settling for a curse word uttered under his breath. The stranger paused again before going on.

"Baudelaire's life was a mess, you know. In certain respects he reminds me of you. How familiar are you with the facts?"

Again the artist did not answer.

"He came from money too," the stranger went on. "When he was very young, his father died, leaving him a substantial inheritance. When Baudelaire came of age and got hold of the small fortune, he started to run through it with total abandon. In no time he would have spent it all on the most absurd extravagances had his mother and her second husband not stepped in. The mother had married again, another man of considerable prominence, who at first was quite willing to use his influence to help young Baudelaire find a suitable position, something secure and enduring. A lot like your father would have done for you. But, of course, he turned all that down, choosing instead his hard and hopeless career in literature. What a miserable life he led, and for what?"

"But look at the body of work he has left us," said Cézanne.

"All the good it did him," sneered the stranger. "He lived miserably, and he died miserably. What kind of life is that?"

"You fool," snapped the artist. "His poetry is proof of how deeply he lived, and his fame today substantiates it."

"Fame that came too late. What's the good of that?

"Fame be damned," returned the artist hotly. "Art and life are not separate. For the artist, at least, making art is life."

"So fame doesn't matter? You don't want recognition? Honors? Sales?"

"Of course I do. Why shouldn't I?"

"Well, dammit, if you don't achieve these while you are alive, then what?"

The artist shrugged. "I have my work...my life."

The confidence and simplicity of Cézanne's answer confounded the stranger. For the first time he felt real anger as he stared at the artist. Cézanne's point of view made no sense to him. The risks and the sacrifices were too great. Toil without reward, in the stranger's mind, was idiocy. The stranger's failure to make Cézanne see this was at the crux of his dilemma. That anything else besides fame and rewards could motivate and sustain the painter was unthinkable to the stranger. Anything else was intolerable.

The impasse between the two men brought on an uneasy silence. Cézanne fell back to studying the still life. The stranger sat down on a chair, the book of poetry still in his hand. With effort, the stranger brought his roiling feelings under control and spoke. "Why don't I read one of the poems out loud while you get into your work there? Don't pay any attention to me. I can't see what you're doing there from here."

The artist said nothing.

"Let's see, what shall it be?"

Cézanne did not even look up as the stranger settled himself more comfortably and started turning the pages of the book.

"Ah, here's one I like: 'Correspondences.' Do you know it?"

Still no sign of recognition from the artist. One could not even be sure if he was listening. The stranger began reading.

"'Nature is a temple, where the living
Columns sometimes breathe confusing speech...'

"'Living columns'...breathing 'confusing speech'? Rather an extravagant image, don't you think? A bit forced, in my judgment."

Abruptly changing his mind, he searched for a different poem.

"No, I know...let me read 'Hymn to Beauty.' He's so gorgeously abandoned...so deliciously reckless...in that one. As if there's no tomorrow. Let's see, it must be here somewhere. Yes, here it is…"

Cézanne spoke up in a firm, clear voice. "'A Carcass'"

"Pardon me," said the stranger, looking up quickly.

"Read, 'A Carcass,'" repeated the artist, now staring straight and hard at the stranger.

The stranger lowered the book to his lap. "Of course, you would choose that! How it ever escaped censure by the authorities is beyond me. They condemned all those others of his, why not that one too? It's so shamelessly disgusting. Yes, by all means, let's read it. I know it's your favorite Baudelaire poem."

Quickly locating the poem and clearing his throat, the stranger began reading. "'A Carcass.' The very title has a certain bite, don't you think? It promises something out of the ordinary. Something unseemly."

He began, "'Remember, my love, the object we saw…'"

"Louder!" said Cézanne.

"All right, all right," said the stranger as he raised his voice. "'Remember, my love, the object we saw

That beautiful morning in June;

By a bend in the path a carcass reclined

On a bed sown with pebbles and stones…'

"It starts right here already…

'Her legs were spread out like a lecherous whore,

Sweating out poisonous fumes,

Who opened in slick invitational style

Her stinking and festering womb…'

"Oh, I like that; it's so outrageous…

'The sun on this rottenness focused its rays

To cook the cadaver till done

And render to Nature a hundredfold gift

Of all she'd united in one.'"

The artist had stopped thinking about his still life and gave his full attention to the words being read by the stranger.

"'And the sky cast an eye on this marvelous meat
As over the flowers in bloom;
The stench was so wretched that there on the grass
You nearly collapsed in a swoon.'"

Cézanne had risen to his feet and joined the stranger, speaking the words from memory. The stranger stopped, and Cézanne went on in a loud voice, heavy with his deep southern accent.

"'The flies buzzed and droned on these bowels of filth
Where an army of maggots arose,
Which flowed with a liquid and thickening stream
On the animate rags of her clothes.'"

Breaking from the poem, the artist suddenly cried, "Damn you and damn them all! Baudelaire's right!" Leaning toward the stranger, he went on excitedly, waving one arm in cadence with the rhythm of the lines. "'And it rose and it fell and pulsed like a wave,
Rushing and bubbling with health.
One could say that this carcass, blown with vague breath,
Lived in increasing itself.'"

The artist was ecstatic; the stranger watched and listened with glee. Then Cézanne stopped reciting and laughed uproariously. "I love Baudelaire! He did not turn away from this object of repugnance. He faced what he had to face, and convention and politeness be damned. He had the balls not only to look at this awful thing but to describe it with utter bluntness. He held back nothing. He did not compromise."

Now the old artist looked down at the still-life objects before him, knowing that he could only paint them by abusing many of the conventions and expectations of others. Thinking still of Baudelaire's daring, he spoke quietly, as if just to himself. "He did not soften it; he did not back away."

Without taking his eyes off the objects on the table, the painter slowly sat down again. His attention now became riveted to the still life, its visual intricacies fully capturing his mind. For the moment the stranger was forgotten and so was Baudelaire.

A silence descended upon the studio once more. The stranger was fascinated by these moods on the part of the artist, who now seemed so transported by his work that he was unaware of anything else around him. The stranger sat quietly watching as the artist continued, unabated, gazing at the still life.

Look at him there, staring at those objects, the stranger thought to himself. *What can he be looking at? What does he see that so engrosses him? Why doesn't he do something? Why doesn't he move? What in heaven's name is he looking at?*

The stranger began to get restless. By just doing his work, the artist not only baffled but irritated the stranger, who took up his book and tried to read silently to himself. It was no use. He looked over again at Cézanne. Nothing had changed. The stranger made some movements, though he did not get up. Nothing. He coughed and cleared his throat. Again nothing. He opened the book of poems and then slammed it shut. Not a stirring from the painter, who continued gazing in rapt contemplation.

The stranger's annoyance was growing, and he was not sure why. But the longer Cézanne stared at his ridiculous objects— those damn apples and that silly jar and pot—the more upset the stranger got. This was absurd! Well, he just was not going to sit there any longer. He got up, put the book down on the empty seat of the chair, and walked warily toward the painter.

Cézanne did not seem to notice him approaching. Standing

off to one side of the table where the still life stood, the stranger bent forward and peered at the arrangement of objects that the painter found so absorbing. Across a bare table a group of red apples lay scattered between an unglazed ceramic pot and a green and white olive jar. A small vase filled with paper flowers stood to one side. As he looked he moved a step closer. Then another step. Without saying a word Cézanne looked up. The painter's sudden and silent recognition was enough to compel the stranger to speak. In a voice louder than was necessary, the stranger asked Cézanne a question. "What are you looking at?"

The simple-minded nature of this question was brought home to the stranger when Cézanne answered it. "I'm looking at my still life."

"Yes, yes," snapped the stranger. "Of course I can see that. But what in particular are you looking at that takes all this time? You've been staring at that same silly apple for fifteen minutes."

"I'm trying to analyze my sensations," replied the artist.

A pause, a frown, and then more questions. "What does that mean? I have sensations. What is there to analyze? Sensations are sensations."

"I'm trying to realize my sensations before nature."

The artist meant this slightly amplified answer in good faith, but it too was lost on his questioner, who only grew more upset. Straining to look harder at the objects on the table, the stranger offered a challenge. "Do you think you see something there that I don't see? I see clearly everything there. The six apples and all the rest. Those peculiar paper flowers, too."

Cézanne pointed to one of the apples. "How many reds do you see? I see nine."

"Nine reds? In that one apple? That's absurd. Why I don't see nine..." His voice trailed off.

Ignoring the stranger's surprise and frustration, the painter said, "That is what I need to get from here to here," pointing to one side of the apple and then the other. "I think it will take nine different reds." And then, on second thought, "Well, at least seven."

The stranger looked utterly confused. This made Cézanne laugh and respond almost jovially. "For somebody who claims to know everything about me, you ask a lot of silly questions."

"Oh, no, no, you misunderstand. I know nothing about your creative side," the stranger hurriedly answered. "Absolutely nothing. I have no access whatever to that part of you. The intentions and the sources of your art are a complete mystery to me."

Hearing this made Cézanne laugh again. "Well it's nice to hear that some part of my life and mind remain my own private affair!"

"Don't be sarcastic."

Cézanne roared again. This little series of triumphs over the stranger seemed to work positively on the artist's disposition; his mood began to brighten.

The stranger tried to explain himself further. "Well, of course, I probably should have told you all this the last time we were together. It just never occurred to me that you wouldn't know that I'm just as much in the dark as everyone else who has no idea what you are doing."

Cézanne's face darkened.

"No, I didn't mean that the way it sounded. I simply meant that your art...you know...it's difficult. It's subtle. And that sometimes you leave us..."

With head lowered and shoulders suddenly sagging, the artist broke in. "I try in my paintings to declare myself clearly and forcefully, but nature presents itself to me in such complex forms that I can express myself only partially. My understanding advances so slowly that I must use paper flowers. Real ones fade and die before I can finish. Sometimes the fruit rots."

"What a maze of contradictions you are! Now this self-effacing humility. Didn't you just tell me a few minutes ago that you were the best of them all?"

Without replying, the artist looked back at his still life. The stranger went on. "You must think me a total dunce about painting. But I know your old Louvre better than you think. I've been there many times. I can tell a portrait by Ingres from one by David."

A peeved look came into Cézanne's face.

"Never mind. You don't have to give me such a pained look. I know perfectly well the low opinion in which you hold Ingres, but there are many who disagree with you. Besides, I know your Delacroix, too, whom I admire as much as anybody. And your Poussin and your Rubens. I know them all. Your Veronese too. How many hours have you spent gazing at his *Marriage at Cana*? Or Puget's *Milo of Crotona*?"

Cézanne stopped working and looked over at the stranger. It was amazing, but this annoying gadfly had done it again. He had just named some of his most beloved artists. These were the chief ones he returned to over the years to study.

"I consider myself a classicist," the stranger intoned. "Give me the Italians every time. The Dutch are too fussy, taken in too much by the specific. Grandeur, that's the ticket. The idealized over the particular any time. Among the Dutch there were exceptions, of course. The older Rembrandt understood this."

Without comment, Cézanne got up and moved away from the still life. He walked to one side of his studio and stood for a moment looking at a very large painting composed of nude female bathers. This work, though well under way, was still far from completed. Certain areas of the canvas were barely touched by any pigment and there were numerous signs elsewhere of parts painted over or painted out. The painting looked as if it had not been worked on for weeks or possibly even months.

The stranger, meanwhile, continued to think about Cézanne's favorite artworks in the Louvre. He especially thought about the larger-than-life marble carved by Pierre Puget of the mythical Milo of Crotona, portrayed in the throes of his terrible death as he was eaten alive by a lion.

"Painting has ravaged your life just as the lion destroyed Milo of Crotona," said the stranger with great scorn in his voice. "At least he had an excuse; he was trapped and could not free himself. But you are not trapped; you voluntarily submit yourself to..."

"No!" shouted the artist.

Cézanne moved quickly toward the stairwell, making as he did so a weary gesture to the other to leave off his lecture. At the head of the stairs the artist turned and descended, leaving the stranger, in an ironic reversal between them, standing perplexed in the middle of the studio. Making his way outside to the terrace, Cézanne walked slowly over to a bench and sat down, deep in thought.

It was still early enough in the morning that the air remained fresh and cool. A group of small birds flew in gay and frenzied pursuit of one another until they disappeared into the foliage of a distant tree. Cézanne barely noticed them as he brooded on the distance he still had to go to achieve clarity in his work. "That idiot is right. My intentions are still not sufficiently clear."

The stranger appeared in the doorway of the studio. He walked to the front edge of the terrace and looked out over the city. Some pots of geraniums were in full bloom along the low wall of the terrace.

"What lovely color," exclaimed the stranger, pointing to the flowers.

Cézanne, whose eyes had followed the stranger's indication, responded petulantly. "Monet should be here to paint that."

"You should paint them yourself."

"No, my art is not about that."

"Nonsense. Stop being so grouchy. Besides, I already know you have painted them."

Before the painter could answer, the bells of Saint-Sauveur rang out, sounding the hour.

"Hmm, nine o'clock," said the stranger. Then for no particular reason, he added, "The new tram to Marseilles will be leaving."

No comment from the artist.

"I hear it makes the trip now in barely two hours. Marvelous, no?"

"I have no interest in that."

"What does that mean?" queried the stranger. "Interest or not, it's quite remarkable that there is such speed and efficiency, don't you think?"

"Oh, I don't know. What good is it? What do we need it for?" persisted the painter. "In my judgment, the old ways were just fine. All these new, so-called improvements strike me as very doubtful in their value. Where will it all lead? This city of my birth"—he gestured toward the town—"is changing before my eyes. I hardly recognize it anymore. I do not like it. I do not approve. I share with Baudelaire...with Delacroix...their hatred of what is called 'progress.' These horseless carriages...these lights that burn all night..."

"So you disapprove of electricity too, do you?"

"Give me the old ways, the old truths. I believe in the unchanging, the eternal, the selfsame..." The artist had risen to his feet; with voice rising, he declared himself with firmness, challenging the stranger to reply.

The stranger could hardly contain himself. He felt a mixture of keen amusement combined with anger. "Really, Cézanne, you are such an irritating riddle. In every respect but one you are utterly unadventurous. In politics, morality, and religion you are as orthodox, traditional, and conservative as anyone. You are a child in good standing in the church. You accept uncritically all the prejudices of your class. And now here you are railing against any sort of social or industrial progress. Yet in your art there are those who assert that you are one of the most original and daring thinkers alive! How to understand this?"

Ignoring the stranger, the painter stood up and looked right past him into the distance. He waved his arm and then sat down again on the bench. The stranger turned to see what had caught the artist's attention. In the distance, a man trudged up the hill toward them.

"It's my gardener, Vallier," said Cézanne blandly.

The stranger started speaking rapidly, saying he was sorry that he suddenly had to leave. He said that he had enjoyed his visit to the studio and that he hoped it was not too stressful or tiring for the artist. Without even giving Cézanne a chance to reply, he had crossed the terrace, passed through the gate, and turned onto the road. In a split second he was gone, the wooden gate thudding shut behind him.

The painter hardly dared believe he was so suddenly freed of his irritating visitor. He stood up and thought of locking the gate as a precaution against the other's return but then remembered that Vallier was coming. Instead, he hurried inside and climbed up the stairs to his studio, all the while thinking of the new things he had to tell his gardener about this latest encounter with the stranger. He had barely reentered his studio when he heard Vallier opening and closing the gate. In another moment, there was the old man coming into view up the stairs.

Before Vallier could even say a word of greeting, the artist pounced on him. "Did you see him, Vallier? Did he talk to you? What did he say? He's the one I told you about...the one who accosted me at the Château Noir. He came back. He came here. He was here this morning when I came in. Can you believe it? Right here in the studio when I arrived. By himself, sitting over there in the corner, just as chatty and at home as you please. Who knows how long he had been here. He'd somehow let himself in. You didn't let him in, did you? Or leave the studio door open? Did you notice how he was dressed? In clothes just like mine! That bore. That thief of my time and patience. He came to spy on me; I'm sure of it. What nerve..."

"Monsieur Cézanne, Monsieur Cézanne!" cried Vallier, who had rarely seen the artist so upset. "What man? What man are you talking about that I saw? I saw no one."

"No one?"

The artist stared incredulously at Vallier.

"Oh yes you did. You must have seen him. He was right there on the road you just came up. He had to pass you. You couldn't miss him. He left just before you arrived. Why, we both saw you from the terrace a few moments ago. It was your coming that seemed to cause him to leave."

"Oh, I'm so sorry, Monsieur Cézanne, but I saw no one. This old head of mine grows worse by the day. I wasn't paying attention. I had things on my mind. One of my daughters is ill and, yes, I stopped on the little bridge to wave to Grégoire, who was at the far end of the Camélia property. This man must have passed by me when my back was turned."

"You didn't see him?" repeated the painter.

Cézanne walked rapidly to the nearest window that gave a view onto the road. He looked out but saw no one.

8

A Long Day in Aix

* * *

Hotel de la Mule Noire
3, Rue Lacépède
Aix-en-Provence

* * *

Wednesday

Dear Maurice,

Greetings from Aix!

Yes, you must be astounded to learn that I am here. I arrived yesterday evening, making the trip at the very last minute. It was a reckless impulse on my part, and I paid the price. I met Cézanne, and our meeting was a disaster!

This all took place late this afternoon, and I'm still beside myself. Now it's after midnight, the air is stifling, and I'm so upset I can't sleep or even remain in bed for long. Since I can't calm down, I'm going to set down on paper everything that has happened to me from the time I decided to come here yesterday. Maybe then, if I get today's events recorded, my mind will surrender to a little sleep. If not, at least I'll have put these odd hours to some good use.

Let me recount things exactly in the order they occurred.

I'm sure you will want to savor every morsel of this story. However much it has devastated me, it must intensely interest you. Even in my present state of mind, I can't fail to see some amusing sides to my ill-fated adventure here. You will recall I thought it unlikely that there would be time left over after my business in Avignon. Well, I was quite wrong about that. The presentation to my father's clients went more smoothly than I could have imagined. I was finished by noon, and they said they would have an answer for me in a day or two...if I didn't mind spending a little time in the town...just until the day after tomorrow...they would arrange excellent accommodations, etc. Can you imagine?

The extra day and a half suddenly made it possible, after all, to think of going to Aix to try to meet Cézanne in person. Given his difficult personality, I knew from the start it was an imprudent idea, especially without warning him. But to tell the truth, I was inspired by Émile's success when he spent a month with Cézanne. If he could have such a wonderful encounter with him, I thought perhaps I could too. To me it would have been worth the trouble if I had only an hour's pleasant conversation with him. And I don't mind admitting that the desire to bring back some new impressions and stories about him to surprise you all was a big part of what prompted me to undertake this escapade. And perhaps doing it all on my own tempted me too.

I walked from the train station to the Hôtel Nègre-Coste, which you may remember Émile recommending. Unfortunately, their rooms were all taken, but they suggested that I try the Hôtel de la Mule Noire nearby, just off Place Forbin. It's a slightly more modest establishment but adequate still in every respect After getting settled in my room, I went to the restaurant—the one Émile found so delicious—where I had an impressive paté de fois gras and the brandade he raved about. How right he was; everything was delightful. Then for dessert I had some pralines and some of the white Grenache from this region. Quite indulgent, I know, but at this point I was feeling very confident and quite satisfied with myself. I foresaw no obstacles to my plan. In fact, after a stroll along the Cours Mirabeau, as if to celebrate in advance my anticipated triumph, I also had coffee and cognac at Les Deux Garçons, the café where Émile had gone a time or two with Cézanne.

Can you see how I was setting myself up? If I were given to making up adages, I would say, in light of what occurred to me today: *Never celebrate an event before it occurs!*

But putting aside that last bit of wisdom learned after the fact, let me return to my state of innocence before the event that was so soon to confront me. Having expressed so many times yourself, Maurice, the desire to meet and converse with him, you can well imagine the excitement and anticipation I was feeling. With Émile's glowing accounts of his meetings with Cézanne still much on my mind, I stared at every tall, old man who passed me by, thinking he might be the one! My memory of him had blurred; I'd seen him only that one time very briefly in Tanguy's shop in Montmartre, and he left almost immediately after we arrived.

Anyway, last night for amusement, I took to asking various people here—the hotel clerk, my waiter, a couple of passers-by on the street—if they knew a Monsieur Paul Cézanne, a native of the town and an artist of fame in Paris. I did not mention the quality of the fame, whether admirable or scandalous, not being sure how extensively Rochefort's vitriolic article on Zola and him had been circulated down here. Of course none of those whom I asked had ever heard of him, although I did find out about a Léonard Cézan who owns a wine shop off La Place des Trois Ormeaux and a Jacques Cézamy who lives in a large house near the Collège Bourbon!

The nearest I got to anything like success came from an elderly gentleman I encountered on the street. He recalled the bank of Cézanne and Cabassol. I knew, of course, that this was Cézanne's father, but then he could think of no one by that name who was, as he described it, an "intellectual!" Can you imagine? But it's not surprising, I suppose, that almost no one down here has heard of him even if this is his hometown. I believe Émile ran into the same difficulty when he first made inquiries after him. After all, what should these fat, prosperous provincials care about the vicissitudes of the Parisian art world? They think that anyone who lives in Paris must be quite mad anyway.

After those first few queries proved so unproductive, I settled for a walk through the town. I thought that if I could find his house, it would save me time when I went to meet him early in the morning.

Without much trouble, I found my way to the charming clock tower that stands in the Place de l'Hôtel de Ville. From there I followed Émile's directions: I took the street to the right that led to Rue Boulegon, walked until I came to number 23, and found Cézanne's house, dark and shut up for the night. Émile had made it clear that Cézanne usually went to bed early; sometimes, if he was especially tired, he retired right after dinner, arising before sunup the next morning in order to get to his painting site with the first light.

At this point there was little left to do. By provincial standards the hour was late; the town was already in bed for the night. Nearly every house was dark and still, just a crack of light here and there around tightly closed shutters. I worked my way back toward my hotel along streets illuminated only infrequently by lamplight but cast everywhere in the pale glow of a full moon. At the hotel I had to knock to get the night porter to let me in.

When I tried to arrange with him to be awakened at 5 a.m., you should have seen this scruffy fellow's face. He had features that were already pinched and drawn, and when he grasped what I was asking him to do, he screwed up his face even tighter. My request clearly was not something that fit into his plans for the night. He was probably used to going to sleep himself in some corner or closet until at least sunup. With cap in hand, he drew his arm across his brow, scratched his neck with long, bony fingers, and shook his head. "Why would anyone want to be up at that hour?" he asked. "There aren't any trains or carriages before 7 a.m. and no businesses open."

When I told him it was none of his damn business why I wanted to get up that early, I saw immediately my mistake. Generally my temper is not my friend in those irritating situations, and this was no exception. It took some stern arguing and a few good sous to get him to consent, grudgingly, to knock at my door at the desired time. These people down here are beyond understanding. You'd think I was asking him to take Prometheus' place on the rock!

You can well imagine my anger when I woke up this morning to sunlight streaming through my window and the sounds of traffic in the street. I leaped out of bed and fumbled for my pocket watch, which—when I opened it—confirmed my worst fears: it was half past eight. That little shit had really done me in!

Of course I should have realized that now there was no need to hurry; Cézanne surely had left his house hours before. But I was so furious that I threw on my clothes, marched downstairs to the desk, and hurled a few choice words at the clerk on duty about what I thought of the night help. He looked apologetically at me from behind the professional mask of sympathy that he had cultivated for just this sort of circumstance, muttered some perfunctory excuse on behalf of the porter, and waited for another blast from me. Realizing the uselessness of making a further fuss, I turned heel and walked out of the hotel.

Without thinking, I started walking toward Cézanne's house. Almost before I knew it, I had crossed the Place de l'Hôtel de Ville and turned down Rue Saint Laurent to Cézanne's street. When I came upon his house again, I was surprised to find it shut up in just the manner in which I'd seen it only a few hours before. It was nearly 9 a.m. by now, more than late enough to expect shutters to be opened and the house to show evidence of a new day's activity. But none of this was apparent, so I didn't even try to arouse anyone by knocking.

Now my anger over my own late awakening gave way to disappointment at the sight of the closed-up house. I had missed my chance to meet him, and suddenly I felt lost and helpless. As I thought this over, I wondered what I was doing there anyway. I was planning to burst in on this man without invitation, introduction, or warning. I would have accosted him in the darkness before daylight; why, I would have come upon him like a thief! What was I thinking? With my innocent but ill-considered plans and hopes caved in, I decided that maybe I was getting what I deserved. I walked slowly back to the square, my mind confused and scattered.

I went on to the first cafe I came to. It was a beautiful, clear morning, and I chose a table on the terrace. I ordered coffee and then leaned back in my chair, feeling really displeased with myself and my situation. Whether I had a right to do so or not, paying my respects, in person, to this man whose art we both love so much was, it seemed to me, well-meaning and a good thing to do, however clumsily I had gone about it.

I sat there pondering whether or not I could dare stay over another day. But how could I meet him? I certainly couldn't approach him tomorrow the way I had planned to do so today. The issue was terminated in my mind when I realized that I should not stay another day. I must return this evening in order to be back in Avignon tomorrow. That decision made, my mood began to lighten. I simply would try to make the best of this disappointing and bungled situation. I looked around me at the others eating and drinking on the terrace, and my own stomach sent up a signal reminding me that I had not yet had any solid food since my indulgent dinner last night. A good breakfast soon diverted the somber focus of my mind.

The morning air was growing warmer, and I glanced up at a blazing sun rising in a cloudless sky. It would surely be another scorching day. Émile is right about the light here in the Midi. Even without a painter's eye, I can see how superb it is. The grey facades of the buildings around the square where I sat had a clarity and presence that I don't remember ever noticing in Paris.

Now my thoughts turned to what I might do to make the best of my first visit to Aix-en-Provence. The museum, of course, was an obvious and easy choice; at least I could do that. I recalled from conversations with Émile that Ingres's gigantic painting of *Jupiter and Thetis* was the star attraction of the permanent collection. That ought to be good for a laugh, I thought to myself. But I couldn't remember if he mentioned any works by Delacroix or Courbet. Probably not. Their work would still be too radical for the likes of a cultural outpost as conservative as Aix. And of course I certainly did not expect to find any paintings by our Impressionist friends, or even Corot.

As I paid my bill, I asked the waiter the way to the museum.

He told me in great detail how to get there, directions which I followed carefully but in a much more leisurely manner than in the hour before when I went so impulsively to Cézanne's house. This time I enjoyed the sights, especially the animated crowds in the markets and around the fountains, of which there are so many here.

Without difficulty I found the Musée Granet next to the church of Saint Jean de Malte. I entered the old building and paid my entry fee. At first no one else seemed to be around. There was just that wonderful silence one experiences in large public buildings. The chance to enjoy this quiet moment, however, was short-lived. I had not taken more than a few steps when I heard a door slam and an angry voice shatter the quiet of the museum. I turned a corner and came upon a rousing scene of bureaucratic bullying. With an air of exaggerated authority, a loud, overbearing man was hotly discussing something with one of the custodians. From the way he talked down to this poor fellow, whom he called Robert, I recognized immediately the haughty demeanor of the petty official. Here was a man utterly self-assured in his superiority talking to another man who he took without question to be his inferior. These types are the same everywhere, and I took a deep dislike to this fellow before a word between us had been exchanged.

As I stood there watching and listening, this bombastic brute noticed me and stopped his harangue long enough to speak to me. He must have seen immediately that I was not a local resident. Waving aside his cringing employee, he stepped toward me, saying directly that I had the honor of being addressed by no one less than the distinguished director of this august institution. I was as amused as amazed and, of course, did my best to look impressed. Without ever having come here, Maurice, I know you have met this fellow.

Facsimiles of him exist everywhere. Daumier has drawn him in a hundred guises, everything from lawyers to bankers to government officials. This type is a petty provincial bureaucrat who is right up Daumier's alley. He is pompous, authoritarian, and rigid. He is surely without imagination.

We exchanged the usual formalities. I told him, with a certain pride of my own, that I was an art collector. I said that I was in Aix only for the day, that I had come from Paris via Avignon, and that I knew there was an important painting by Ingres in the museum here. From all this he construed that I had made the trip here for the sole purpose of seeing his *Jupiter and Thetis*. At the very mention of the painting, you could see his pride swell.

At this point, the poor man who he had been castigating muttered a word or two, half bowed, and turned to leave in a hurry. I was glad to have rescued this abused fellow, though I had little doubt that it would be no more than a momentary respite for him. Meanwhile, Monsieur le Directeur had not paid the slightest attention to his departing worker. He was already full of himself, gesturing grandly in the direction in which I assumed his masterpiece was exhibited. He extolled the painting in superlative terms, assuring me that it was the greatest work by a French artist, not just in Aix but in the entire Midi. Imagine that if you can!

He offered to escort me personally to where his masterpiece resided, bidding me to follow him down a corridor. As we went along, he effusively pointed out various works in the collection—the head of a man by Jordaens here, an admirable portrait by Philippe de Champaigne there. He urged me to see the Italian primitives and the Granet legacy upstairs, which included more works by Ingres, not the least of which, so he assured me, was a superb portrait of Granet himself by the master. We paused before a charming portrait of a young boy by David, which he rapturously praised.

This talkative fellow wore his tastes and his aesthetics like medals on his chest. To say he was out of touch by several decades would be no exaggeration, though there are still plenty of hopelessly conservative people in the Parisian art world who would agree with him. Why, I wouldn't be surprised if this man still has reservations about Delacroix, even though he has been dead for more than thirty years!

It's as if his awareness and certainly his artistic loyalties stopped well before the Commune. He has no idea that the battle he is fighting has long since been over. Here in this isolated museum he is like an entrenched soldier who hasn't heard that the war has ended. In his exaggerated praise of even the most insipid pieces of the classical school, and at the expense of anything obviously derived from our beloved Delacroix, he declares his position. If his pomposity hadn't been so comical, he would have been unbearable. He had all the rhetorical flourishes down perfectly. Listening to him babble on was awful, and finally he got to me. His bombast overpowered the comedy I first saw, and the more he talked the more upset I became, though to this point I had said nothing to disturb his calm assurance that I was one of his own. As he droned on, I searched in my mind for some way to irritate him, if not make him outright angry at me. I wanted at least to find something to say, something he would find exasperating.

We were standing in front of Ingres' huge, utterly boring picture, the light so bad we could see it only with difficulty, when the impulse to act came over me.

"I adore Manet, don't you?"

The words struck him like a slap in the face. His smile froze; his eyes widened. He started to say something like, "That imposter. But surely you don't mean..."

And then I had to hand it to him; he bit off the end of his own sentence and within the instant sized me up as a member of the other camp. What a moment that was between us. As I think of it now, there was something unreal and theatrical about it; in that large and stately space, it was as if we were actors in an operetta. He glared at me, and I returned an icy gaze back at him. The rage that poured into his face might have been as much at himself as at me. After all, he had allowed himself to escort someone who was, for him, the enemy across his own turf to a place in front of what he viewed as the holy of holies. He quickly collected himself, a look of cold reserve recapturing his features. He bowed stiffly, as if his body were dipped in starch, and in the most detached tone possible dismissed me. Then he strode off, his upper torso to the height of his lower lip, arched in tension. You can imagine my amusement; I could hardly contain myself.

Before he was out of sight, though, I was tempted for a second time by the most delicious possibility. I was positive that I had one more salvo that would surely cause huge mischief. In a voice as innocent as I could make it, I called after him asking if he had any works in his museum by a Monsieur Paul Cézanne!

The name struck him in the back like a dagger. He stopped, wheeled around, and gave me a scowl that would have frightened Medusa. I can assure you that matters were not improved when I added, "Monsieur Cézanne is a native of your beautiful city and resides here to this very day."

I could never have anticipated what followed. He clenched one hand tightly into a fist and buried it with all his force into the other hand, making the snapping sound of skin sharply hitting skin. As he did this, he spoke in a voice that grew louder with almost every word. "No!' I'll never permit it. Never! Never! As long as I am director of this museum, no abomination by that incompetent fool will ever enter this collection. What he calls art is ridiculous. It is an absurdity. Look, you fool, at this great painting in front of you by our heroic Ingres. This is art! Your Cézanne is utterly without talent; he cannot draw a line or paint a stroke that has true artistic worth. Away with him! Away with you!"

He pronounced these words as if they were an oath, spoken not just to me but to the whole world. This time when he stalked off, I did not deter him but stood there myself, open-mouthed and stunned by this expression of anger and hatred. Even more than his words, the tone of his voice expressed such a deep and uncontrolled loathing. At the time I heard him, it went beyond amusing. This was a man emotionally unhinged, suddenly discharging some deeply held-back feelings that now burst forth like an explosion. It was scary to behold. It would be some time before I saw a comical side to all this. The moment after he left, I felt shaken and—I must admit—relief from a slight feeling of fright. His rant held an edge of threat.

The very last thing I heard from him was a loud cry, "Robert!" and then a door slamming. I'm afraid poor old Robert was in for far worse than when I first came upon him. How I wish you or some of the others had been there with me. You would have eaten him alive in one gulp, Maurice.

As I think about it now, these many hours later, it's possible to see how this tormented man has become so closed and hostile to the more recent art. He must, after all, have some awareness that art has evolved. He probably senses that something is going on in more recent art, but he doesn't know what it is, and this threatens him. Living here as he does in this distant place, well out of the mainstream, he's rarely exposed to the raw force of new ideas. He's locked away in his little museum, where he presides over an art collection formed by the sensibility of a past era. He has a personal stake, an identity, in the continuance of that aesthetic. Even if he could, he dare not take Cézanne seriously. He is utterly without the intellectual resources to comprehend Cézanne's intentions or, seemingly, even those of his colleagues and their immediate predecessors.

But why am I apologizing for him? Dammit, he's a fool! Cézanne is a treasure in his midst, and he's totally incapable of realizing that. Anyway, what an encounter, eh? I'll not soon forget it.

Right after he left, I stood there almost numb. I went over to a stone bench where I sat for a few moments. My mind was torn between laughing at this stupid man and feeling sorry for him.

Then my eye settled on the great painting across from me. *Jupiter and Thetis* had borne witness to the event too! My imagination, almost against my will, started to play. I saw the look on the dour face of the god as he sat so stiffly on his throne. His gaze seemed to accuse me of unfairly attacking his warrior, who I had just sent storming off the battlefield. The half-naked body of Thetis, so flat it seemed boneless, slithered up the side of the stern god's torso, making the effect all the more bizarre. She was at his side pleading for his favors while I was abusing one of his ardent supporters right in front of his face!

What foolishness, right?

You will understand that after the encounter with this angry bureaucrat, I was not fit to look at another picture. I made my way out of the empty museum, passing the custodian at the door who had taken my entry fee such a short time before. He stared at me wide-eyed as I departed out into the bright sunlight. He must have been astounded at the shouting he had surely heard.

Once outside, the brightness and the heat took over. My appetite was suddenly up and roaring; I was famished. But as attractive as the thought of eating was, I decided to make one more pass by Rue Boulegon to see if by chance Cézanne had turned up. Upon regaining his street, I found all of the shutters open and even some of the windows.

Good heavens, he's in there right now! I thought.

I stood off to the side for a couple of minutes, collecting myself. Then I went up to the front door and knocked. A stern-looking woman opened the door cautiously and regarded me with a suspicious stare. She was wearing a full blue dress tied tightly at her waist by a cloth belt. Several vertical pleats from her shoulders to her waist articulated the upper part of her garment, which had long sleeves and a collar tied snugly around her neck. In defiance of the heat, she was buttoned up tightly, and her braided hair—pulled back closely in a ring at the back of her head—only added to her strict and businesslike air. I wondered at first if she were Madame Cézanne and then decided otherwise.

First I enquired if indeed this was the residence of Monsieur Cézanne, the artist. With a curt nod she acknowledged that it was. Then I quickly introduced myself, making sure to say right off that besides being an admirer of the painter, I was a good friend of Émile Bernard. Émile's name produced a perceptible relaxation of her body and a smile of recognition and pleasure. She told me that her name was Madame Brémond, the Monsieur's housekeeper. She asked if Émile were also here and how his wife was, etc., sending best wishes when she realized he was not here with me. Then she told me, regretfully, that her employer was not here. She had not, in fact, seen him since the day before yesterday and didn't quite know when to expect him back. She said he was working at the Château Noir. At the puzzled look on my face, she told me it was a large house about a mile outside of town on the road to Le Tholonet.

Yes, she thought that I would probably be able to find him there. No, she didn't think it would be an imposition if I went to see him since I was a friend of Monsieur Bernard's. So after getting a few more words of instruction about how to find my way, I left Madame Brémond, who wished me good luck and reminded me again to send her regards to Émile and his wife.

I walked slowly back along the route I had just come, pondering my options. Beneath my turmoil was a clear urge to resume my quest to meet this man whom we so admire, Maurice, and I quickly rationalized my ability to do this with plenty of time to get back to Aix in order to catch the evening train. This matter settled, I quickened my step and set out immediately to find the road to Le Tholonet.

As I crossed the town once more, I came upon some shops on the Rue Thiers, where I purchased some bread, cheese, fruit, and a bottle of wine. I didn't dare take the time to stop for a proper meal. I would simply eat something on the roadside along the way. For the moment, though, I only wanted to get out of town and be well on my way.

The city rapidly gives way to the country as soon as one sets out to the east of Aix. At a certain turn in the road, Cézanne's mountain looms up like a vast sentinel. Before that, there is just a scattering of houses among lovely almond and olive groves mingled with cypresses, after which one moves into pine forests. The road rises and falls a good deal and turns often. The color today was superb. You may remember Émile telling us about the extraordinary red-orange hue of the earth in these parts; well, it's an even deeper, richer tone than I had anticipated. Émile is right: the local color in many of Cezanne's landscapes is more like the color of the actual terrain here than anyone who has never seen this country could possibly imagine.

At one place, I suddenly came upon an extraordinarily beautiful vista. Two umbrella pines flanked the curving road, and above them I saw the best view yet of Mont Sainte-Victoire. I noticed a little path on the hill to my left that I climbed for a short distance in order to get above the road on which I was travelling. I made this little detour hoping for even a better view still, and it was breathtaking. There was a surge to the mountain as it abruptly rose above the irregular curves of the dark green trees between which the road below turned and disappeared around a bend. In the clear blue brightness and the heat, the angular contour of the mountain seemed magnified. Its mass had a kind of hypnotic power as it loomed above the trees below me and filled the space formed by the limbs from another group of nearby trees above me. A lone farmhouse stood out vividly in the distance, enfolded in the green forest at the base of the mountain. I even imagined that this very place where I stood could be a site where Cézanne might paint the spectacular scene that spread out before me.

I have never felt closer to Cézanne than at that moment. I was able to grasp in a new way how much the spirit of this countryside resides in him and he in this countryside.

Before leaving this beautiful sight, I ate some of the cheese and bread I had brought along and drank a little wine. Then I went back down on the road and proceeded a short distance further to what I thought must be my destination, the Château Noir. I passed a smaller house in the chateau park and then came to a cistern next to what seemed an abandoned project for a mill. Cut rock lay strewn about, and there was an old mill wheel standing on its end. At the time, I hardly paid attention to what lay there before me; little did I know that in a few moments I would be back there studying the site intently.

I finally arrived at the terrace of the main building itself. This structure, as I soon found out, was composed of two wings around a courtyard, only partly connected by an unfinished orangery. I entered the courtyard without seeing anyone. The place looked run-down; parts of it almost took on the aspect of a ruin, a condition peculiarly enhanced by a row of unfinished columns supporting nothing but air. In the middle of the courtyard, there was a pistachio tree that seemed to be growing out of some heavy blocks of stone loosely stacked in a square. Beside the tree lay a thick, rounded stone that looked as if it could have been a lid for a well, though as far as I could tell there was no well nearby.

As I stared at this odd grouping of objects before me, which looked as if it were a still-life composition waiting to be painted, an old woman carrying a bucket came into the courtyard from out of the main wing. She didn't notice me immediately, and the first sounds of my voice startled her.

I apologized for not having called out sooner and then told her who I was looking for. Without speaking, she looked me up and down for several seconds. Finally she asked where I was from and what made me think I'd find him here. I told her that Madame Brémond had sent me and that while I did not yet know Monsieur Cézanne personally, I was a great admirer of his painting and had a friend in common with him. I was about to mention Émile's name when she let out a snicker and asked if I thought he was a great painter. The edge of defiance in her voice signaled her position, so when I answered that, indeed, I thought he was a great artist, her scoffing reply did not surprise me.

"Him? A great artist? That's a good one. He's a laughing-stock in town, you know."

I tried immediately to change the subject by saying

something nice about the courtyard, but she totally ignored me and went on about Cézanne. "I've heard that young kids throw stones at him, the brats. They ought to be whipped, if you ask me. Oh, he's odd all right. But he never bothers anybody. He just goes up there into the rocks above the house or on the paths around here, painting for hours those queer pictures of his."

Since she seemed willing enough to talk about him, I asked if by chance he were anywhere around right now. Ignoring me again, she went on, "The day before yesterday he was down the path there painting away for hours in front of that old millstone. Now why would he paint a thing like that? It's such an old, dirty thing, and it's just leaning against a rock with a lot of other rocks around it. There's not even a mill there. It never got built. It's ugly, if you ask me."

I tried to find out how long he had been working on the painting of the millstone. She started to bend down over her bucket and then paused, her thoughts about Cézanne gathering their own momentum. "He rents from me, you know." She straightened up and pointed to a second-floor window behind me. "He even tried to buy my place once. He made me an offer two or three years ago, but I wouldn't sell. Then he came back one day and rented that room from me to store his painting things in. And sometimes he sleeps there, too. Sometimes he's around here for days or else up in the rock quarry where he is now."

Damned, if I didn't miss him again! "Is that far from here?" I asked.

She replied, "Up on the ridge," and as she pointed vaguely behind her, she shook her head to indicate that it was not far. Then, in this strange, disconnected way she had of thinking, she returned to what for her was another irritating anecdote about Cézanne. "You know, he left the painting of the millstone leaning up against the banister of the stairway over there. I nearly walked into it this morning." She made another vague gesture, this time toward the door in the wing where she had indicated Cézanne's room was. "He could do better than leave his work lying around in a person's way. My grandson has found his paintings lying on the ground or even hanging in the trees with him nowhere around. What do you think of that? He just throws them away when he gets into one of those rages of his. He really is a queer duck, if you ask me."

Then she poured out the contents of her bucket into a gutter and stood up to leave.

"Madame, could you tell me how to get to the quarry from here?"

She pointed out a path that she said crossed the Jesuit property that bordered hers. The Domaine Saint-Joseph, she called it. She said I should follow the little path there, always being sure to take the route up the hill whenever I came to a fork. I would come to a groundskeeper's cottage along the way and should ask for further directions if I needed them. I tried to thank her as she disappeared into the wing from which she had emerged, but she paid me no attention.

The sun beat hot patches of light onto the pavement of the courtyard, and I sat for a few moments on the warm stones that surrounded the pistachio tree. So now I was supposed to climb a steep hill up to a rock quarry. Well, why not! My little adventure was turning into a saga, so why should I interrupt its flow? I stood up and was about to head in the direction of the Jesuit property when I thought of the canvas by Cézanne the old woman told me was leaning against a railing inside the doorway. I couldn't resist this chance to see a new work in progress.

I crossed the courtyard, looked around to see if anyone

was watching, and went in at the door she had indicated. At first, my sudden passage from the bright light outside into the cool darkness of the stairwell made it hard to see. But when my eyes adjusted, I saw the canvas tipped up on its side at the foot of the stairway. I wondered how he could have left it in such an odd place. There was an old jacket lying beside it. I took the painting outside into the bright light and propped it up against the pistachio tree. Work on this piece was well advanced, and how stunning it was!

The slender trunks of two pairs of trees tipped at consecutively steeper angles as they moved from right to left across the middle of the painting. They divided the horizontal canvas into a series of vertical sections in alternating rhythms of wide and narrow. In the extreme lower left foreground the old millstone stood straight up on its edge as if it were a giant cartwheel. Its strong circular form focused everything; even the nearest pair of trees seemed to bend toward it.

In the middle ground two boulders, their axes tipping toward the mill wheel, were interspersed among the pairs of trees. Below one of them lay heaped a haphazard pile of irregular stones. Moving diagonally into the painting from the lower right corner were a scattering of four or five long blocks of cut stone about the size and shape of heavy windowsills or cornices. Their squared geometry along with the clear and distinct circular shape of the millstone contrasted dramatically with the irregularity of the uncut rock. Critical to the structure of the picture were shadow patterns that linked the elements of trees and stones together in angular zones. Everything was held in the most delicate and precarious equilibrium, as if a breeze could not arise without upsetting the fragile balance or one more patch of light appear without endangering the stability of the composition.

It struck me how interesting it would be if I took this

painting to the very site where he painted it. I knew I had passed the place on my way into the chateau grounds. No one was around, so I gingerly picked up the canvas and quietly headed off in the direction from which I had entered the property. I came upon the place again in moments. With the painting as my guide, I maneuvered myself around to where he must have stood. I looked for signs that he had been there and, in fact, found some tiny specks of oil color on a twig at my feet. With the aid of a stick, I propped up the painting and then backed off a few steps in order to better view the site and the painting together. What a fascinating study for me!

The light was not right; the shadows in the painting were different, but everything else was there in place. I guess what surprised me the most was the degree to which he had submitted himself to what was before him. He left out very little of that part of the site he chose here to paint, and yet everything was subtly transformed by the way he rendered it. He did omit the cistern to the right, which was surprising because it seemed like such a prominent element in the setting. But as I think now about his choice in that regard, it must have had something to do with the particular responses of his sensibility. Perhaps the cistern to one side and the mill wheel to the other split up a kind of focus he wanted. In any case, perhaps he plans to return here and paint a version of the scene that favors the cistern. Who knows?

I made an effort, Maurice, to remember what you explained to me about his insistence on the motif. With his painting as my eyes, I attempted to reconstruct from the natural, extended scene what in particular had captured his attention. One of the obvious qualities here was the play between the living organic rock and the geometrically carved blocks, including especially the perfectly round wheel of stone. The more I looked at what Cézanne had done, the more I realized that this quasi-architectural concern expressed by the cut stones was carried out in another way throughout the whole composition of the picture. The three large vertical spaces formed by the pairs of trees suddenly seemed susceptible to a kind of architectural description, even though they were a part of the natural landscape. Within the borders of the composition, these spatial divisions were like bays or openings through which one could see. Even though tipped to the left, the trunks of the two sets of trees functioned in the manner of paired columns!

I could have spent much more time here with the painting, studying it in comparison with its actual site in nature. But then I realized that if I were going to go through with this little enterprise of mine—the finding of Cézanne—I needed to put this wonderful pleasure aside and get on with my search. So I carefully picked up the canvas—the paint was still wet, you understand—and walked back to the courtyard, which was as deserted as when I had left it twenty minutes earlier. There was neither sight nor sound of Madame. Putting the painting back where I had found it was quickly done, and I was off in the direction of the Jesuit property that would lead, I hoped, to the rock quarry beyond it.

An opening in a low stone wall brought me to a steep slope. The red-tiled roofs of some buildings below me were visible through the trees, no doubt those of the religious community itself. As instructed by Madame, I kept to the high paths, and soon a small cottage came into view, which I took to be the groundskeeper's residence. I decided to knock and ask for clarification of my directions, since I didn't have a very clear idea of where I was going or a whole lot of time to waste. It was getting toward midafternoon when I knocked on the half-open door of the little house.

In a moment, a slightly built woman in her middle years

with dark eyes, deeply tanned skin, and long, jet-black hair appeared in the doorway. Her feet were bare and she wore a simple tunic tied loosely at her waist. A faded pattern of large flowers was strewn through her garment. She looked care-worn and tired, but there was a gentleness in her features and she carried herself with an erect dignity. She nodded in response to my greeting and asked in low tones what I wanted. As I started to speak, she abruptly put her forefinger to her lips, urging me to lower my voice. She nodded behind her as if there were someone inside the cottage whom she didn't want disturbed. I resumed speaking in a whisper and had barely finished making my request for directions when a male voice from within asked her who was there. At the sound of his calling to her, she frowned anxiously, half curt-sied to me and, without another word, withdrew quickly into the darkness of the room, leaving the door ajar.

From inside I heard loud, incomprehensible whispers and the sounds of movements as if someone were hurriedly dressing. The voices were so muffled I wasn't even sure if they were speaking our native tongue.

In another moment or two, the door to the cottage was opened wide, and through it stepped a robust, brightly smil-ing man of medium height and middle age. His short, curly hair, with traces of white, still retained much of its original black color, as did his bushy eyebrows. He greeted me effu-sively, speaking with a charming accent full of the drawl of this southern region of our country. Certain inflections in his speech still bore traces of what were surely his Italian origins. In spite of his cordial manner, I sensed that he was intently looking me over and rapidly sizing me up, though for what purpose I did not know.

He was dressed only in trousers, sandals, and an under-shirt, causing me to think he had just gotten up from a nap. The time of day was right, it being toward the end of the siesta hour. His olive skin reflected the healthy look of someone who spends much time out of doors. His arms were strong and lean, his shoulders broad, and his barrel chest well defined beneath his thin undershirt. He was clean-shaven about the chin but sported a marvelously flowing moustache. The numerous laugh wrinkles about his eyes suggested someone who enjoyed the pleasures of life. Most memorable was a wonderful pipe he carried in one hand, its bowl carved into the head of a fantastical horned beast.

You must get the idea by now, Maurice, that I was quite taken with this fellow who suddenly appeared before me out of the darkness of his small cottage. And to describe him a little more, his face seemed cast in a perpetual smile and he had a slow, very deliberate way of speaking, frequently punctuated by a kind of deferential laughter. With neither fanfare nor curiosity about my request, which obviously had been relayed to him by the woman who I thought now was probably his wife, he announced that he was going to take me personally up the hill to the quarry.

"It is my pleasure, Monsieur, to guide you to the very best place where you can enter the quarry."

When I tried to tell him it was hardly necessary and that I could find my own way, he waved aside my protests and called for his shirt. His wife had been standing in the shadows of the doorway, and now she silently disappeared into the cottage only to reemerge a moment later with a shirt that she handed to her husband, whispering something in their native language as she did so.

He slowly donned the garment, leaving the front unbuttoned, then he drew from a pocket of his pants a black pouch, into which he thrust his pipe. With slow and practiced movements, he carefully filled the bowl with tobacco and tamped it down. This process was done in absolute silence and with such gentle and loving care that for a moment I was transfixed watching him. His concentration was totally focused on this small task. Only when he had finally placed the stem of the unlit pipe between his lips and found that it drew properly did he look up, the smile on his face expressing his satisfaction. He did not light the pipe immediately; instead, he closed up the tobacco pouch and, as he returned it to his pocket, told to his wife in a soft, lilting French that he would be back before sundown. When I heard that, I thought to myself, *My God, how far away is this place?* Only when he told her he would return by way of the lower road where he had some work to do, did I hope that my leg of the journey might be short.

Standing there waiting for him to lead me up the hill, I had no idea what was coming. I was about to enter into an experience with him that I neither expected nor for which was I in the least prepared. I thanked his wife and said good-bye; he nodded to her and waved to me to follow him. As we slowly took our first few steps up the narrow path to our left, she turned back toward the house, waving to us as she went. Almost immediately, the path we were on changed direction and a stand of pines obscured our view of her and the cottage, so we turned fully to face the steep slope ahead of us, my Italian escort in the lead with me close behind.

Our very first point of attack consisted of stopping while he deliberately lit his pipe. Only after the pipe drew to his satisfaction did we face the hill again, this time actually getting ourselves under way. The manner of our progress was most remarkable, Maurice, and deserves a brief explanation. This curious man walked to a rhythm not of this time. He moved as if all the ages were in him, as if he were the inhabitant of another zone of existence. We moved at a pace so slow that we might as well have been down on all fours!

During the first several minutes of our progress, I could only think there was something amiss, that something was not quite right and he was settling the matter in his mind before we strode off. But I was forced very quickly to realize that this was not the case at all. We were walking at precisely the tempo he desired. We walked so slowly it took me several tries to get myself sufficiently slowed down so that I could walk in unison behind him, while at the same time looking around me.

Besides our extreme slowness of step, we also paused often. We would walk a short distance, when he would stop to point out something or else just to talk and to view the panorama unfolding around us. We were climbing a steep slope toward a thus-far invisible point somewhere on the ridge above us. The forest was thick where we walked, though from time to time there would be gaps allowing us a charming view of the slope across the valley. Trees on the hills opposite were thinner, and we could see small patches of terraced farmland and vineyards interspersed with cottages and stone walls. It was very beautiful and reminded me of paintings by Cézanne, Pissarro, and the others.

When we paused to survey the countryside, my Italian companion (by some odd oversight, we never did exchange names, you know) told me stories about his life here, especially his youth. He was born in Genoa but said he came here when he was very young, less than ten years old. I gathered that he had lived his whole life here since arriving in these hills, isolated for the most part even from the slow-paced urbanization of Aix, which he told me he did not care for and visited infrequently. He seemed to know everything about the countryside and pointed out places on the opposite slope where, as a boy, he had tended sheep. He claimed to have walked many times on every trail and path in the countryside.

Indeed, he said that over the years he had maintained a lot of them, and by this time I had no reason to doubt. He could have told me he had laid out each pathway with his own hands, and I would have believed him. It was as if he had a deep acquaintance with the state and disposition of every object, organic and inorganic, around him.

After a while, walking at this slow gait began to drain away my nervous energy, and I reached a calmer state. I began to take stock of my situation. Progressing up our hill at a snail's pace, time ceased to matter. I noticed how beautiful our surroundings were. It was the hottest time of day, and while the heat bore down on us even through the tree cover, our tempo protected us from its worst effects. I found that I was slowly being drawn out of myself by the charm of this man. It was clear that he had developed an intimately focused relationship with this physical world in which he lived, and I began to want to know it through him.

After all, what else could I do? He was really being very generous, though I had no doubts that he would be looking for some token of my gratitude for his time and trouble. But finally, almost as if he were working a spell on me, I fell into his rhythm in mind as well as body. I turned myself over to my imperturbable guide, letting him lead me for the duration at whatever pace he would. Throughout our climb together I said very little. He talked and gestured; I listened and looked on. On one of the few occasions I ventured to speak, I asked him if he knew Cézanne. Interestingly enough, he did not know him by name, but when I mentioned what he did and told him that he often worked in the woods near here as well as up in the quarry where we were heading, he knew exactly who I was talking about. He smiled and said that he had seen him just a couple of days before around the Château Noir. Then, when I said that the reason I was going to the rock quarry was to try to find him, he just turned and looked at me without saying a word.

After this exchange, we proceeded on for some distance in silence, our pace remaining at the same slow, unvarying rate. After a while, my steadfast attention to my guide began to ebb. I took more cognizance of what was happening to me and my surroundings in a new and interesting way. I became aware of the swaying of my body as we walked and the effect this had on how I experienced what I saw around me. As we slowly passed through the randomly spaced trees, dense and numerous around us, the trunks seemed to be in motion, rocking in harmony with the movement of my body. I watched with fascination the trees nearest our path as they passed in front of those farther away. Have you ever noticed the phenomenal changes that occur to the spaces between trees when you walk by them, Maurice? They are continually expanding and shrinking.

Of course, all these experiences occur at whatever pace one keeps. But at a normal walk, who would ever bother to notice such useless phenomena? It was as if this extremely slow walking had disengaged me from my normal patterns of awareness. The slowing down of my body brought up a different sensitivity and mind-set, and this little event of my bodily movement became suddenly very evident and fascinating to observe.

The nearest memory I have that parallels this experience was when I was a child and hunted tiny seashells and colored stones on the gravelly beach where my parents summered. My little sister and I would slowly walk over long stretches of the beach in search of our bounty. The shells and pebbles we sought were often so tiny that we had to proceed with an unnatural slowness just to see them at all.

But here and now with my Italian guide, I looked above

our heads into the maze of foliage, which at times was so dense the sunlight barely penetrated it. I became intrigued by the tracery-like effects of the tree branches that arched and bent in infinitely varied ways. This is the stuff from which Cézanne makes his paintings, and I fancied that I saw his subjects everywhere. Here was a branch that gracefully reached out in a series of splendid curves, repeated and reinforced by another branch on a nearby tree.

In a group of trees where each was set at a slightly different interval from the others, I saw an exquisite series of branches breaking up and enlivening with great delicacy the spaces between the trunks. The whole was set against a screen of gauzy, green bushes and other foliage, relieved here and there by patches of orange-colored earth that rose up behind. I noticed things on the ground near me. It seemed as if I could see the edges of every blade of grass, the texture on every stone, and the shape of every flower. I watched with keen attention as we approached a boulder next to our path. I found myself enjoying the intricacy of the faceted surfaces of the rock as one plane passed into the next. I could have gone on like this indefinitely. At this pace our steady climb, quite steep at times, was effortless. Truly, Maurice, the physical exertion was minimal. Had I been here on my own, by now I would have been huffing and puffing and hell-bent on getting to the ridge, having seen little or nothing along the way. But with him, I was drawn into intently watching all about me, and the unhurried time I had for doing this was crucial to my being able to do it at all.

We'd been climbing for well over an hour when my new-found friend turned to me and pointed to a couple of large pines above us toward which our path was leading. "The ridge of the hill, Monsieur, is just beyond those pines over there, and the quarry begins right after that. Just follow the old road, and you will see some of the diggings."

His smile expressed his satisfaction for what he had just done. Then he told me he would leave me there at the ridge. So just beyond the two trees at the top of the hill, we stopped together for the last time. He pointed out the route I should follow, cautioning me that the quarry diggings, which had been abandoned for years, were scattered here and there over a fairly large area and that many of them, mined down into the ground, were easily missed because of tree and brush cover. As for finding Cézanne, he merely shrugged. He had no specific suggestions. As I thanked him, he beamed at me his ever-charming smile. My gratitude was genuine. I knew all along that he had done more for me than just getting me to the edge of the quarry; my time with him, though brief, was memorable, and I would not soon forget it. We shook hands vigorously and I pressed upon him a gratuity that at first he feigned to resist but eventually accepted, and I was glad he did. Thus we parted, waving to each other.

I proceeded along the path, which was now level, while he dropped back down the side of the hill we had just climbed. After he was gone, I turned to face the path that at this point had come out of the forest momentarily into a clearing. It was so quiet I nearly held my breath. The heat beat down on me, the brightness of the sunlight was intense, and no breeze stirred. The beauty of the landscape was enhanced by the great silence in which it was immersed. In the moments immediately following my Italian's departure, I felt filled with an exhilaration and sense of peace that I will not soon forget.

The sound of my own steps on the rocky earth was clear and strangely magnified. Without willing it, I began to walk faster. It was as if some impulse in my body wanted to restore a more natural pace. Without my Italian guide there to hold me in check, I returned to the zone where I habitually live.

I decided to sit in the shade of a nearby tree to collect my thoughts and have something more to eat. A glance at my watch told me that in barely two hours I had to start back to town if I wanted to catch my train. My chances at this point of finding Cézanne were slim, and I all but gave up on the idea. I began to think that just the pursuit itself this day proved to be a sufficiently interesting adventure, even without reaching my goal. I was content to let it go at that.

But you will soon see how wrong I was!

My thoughts turned once more to the Italian. I tried to picture his life here, especially its tempo in this remote and beautiful place. I don't think I have ever met anyone more at home in his surroundings. His pace was as slow and steady as this countryside is harmonious and eternal.

As I sat there trying to understand what had happened to me because of this strange man, I recalled a conversation with Émile about his visit with Cézanne. You will recall that he had even made a room beneath his studio available to Émile so he could also paint. Émile told me that more than once when he was working there he heard Cézanne above him slowly pacing back and forth in front of his easel for long periods of time. I imagined my Italian and me walking at that same pace!

***

As I glance back over what I have written here, I'm amazed at its length. Indeed, as this letter attests, this has been a day densely packed with a variety of experiences. Now as I look out of my hotel window, I realize that dawn has come and gone without my noticing. There is nearly full light outside, and I just heard two people talking in the street below my window. I have been awake all night, and still I cannot sleep.

At least I am much calmer. But let me not dally; before I stop, I must bring my little narrative to its rousing climax.

***

In the hour following the Italian's departure, I mostly wandered along the main path across the plateau that contained the Bibémus Quarry. What I soon found myself following seemed more like an old abandoned road than a path. It was probably the route along which the quarried stone had once been hauled. I got off this road just once and then not for long, as I didn't want to lose my bearings. It seemed to me that getting lost would not be difficult and that finding my way again would not be easy.

My Italian guide was certainly right to tell me that the quarry diggings were hard to find. They were openings cut randomly in step fashion into the ground, mostly hidden from view by trees and bushes. Though there were probably many others, I found only three places where there had been extensive excavations, and what glorious architectures they formed. The ocher stone—which by turns showed itself in versions of red, orange, and brown—was arbitrarily cut in a dizzying array of geometric blocks. There seemed to be no logic to the way the rock was worked or any reason it was abandoned in the strange forms in which I found it. In the process of the digging, wonderful structures—shapes like towers, bridges, and caves—had been carved and then forsaken, left to the weather and the few living flora that managed to grow up in the clefts and other barely hospitable gaps and cleavages. The evergreen foliage of laurel, thyme, and rosemary played strikingly against the warm tones of the geometrically cut stone.

As I wandered through this beautiful place, my feeling of

peace continued. Yes, I walked slowly, though not quite at the pace of the Italian, I admit. Yet the mood he had evoked still clung to me, and I was grateful for it. I finally decided to sit for a while, since by now the thought of finding our elusive painter had all but disappeared from my mind.

I chose a place in front of several high boulders that stood side by side, shaded from the late afternoon sun by a row of trees behind them. It was my intention to sit there for a while before starting back to Aix. I can't say exactly when I fell asleep or how long it was before a series of fiercely shouted curses broke upon my sleep, causing me to jump to my feet in a state of terror. I looked frantically around me but saw no one. The cursing had stopped as suddenly as it had begun, and I was surrounded again by silence. I began to wonder if I had been dreaming when another round started up, just as loud as before.

"Too damn much blue!..."

"That's a fucking purple in that rock!..."

"It can't be done!..."

I was now fully awake and could pinpoint the direction from which these wild words arose; the speaker was some-one located on the other side of the tall boulders I had just been leaning against. Again the cursing stopped and com-plete silence prevailed.

As quietly as I could, I moved up to the obstruction of rocks between me and the mystery person on the other side. I found a narrow foothold by which I could raise myself to a sufficient height and carefully peered through a dense screen of foliage just beyond my stony perch.

The trees through which I looked were on the edge of a small clearing. He stood slightly to my left, his back to me. We were barely ten or twelve feet apart. His portable easel was directly in front of me, poised delicately on its slender legs. My line of sight permitted me a clear, unimpeded view of the canvas that stood on the easel. I needed no other corroborating evidence to identify this man: he was painting a Cézanne!

I was so startled I nearly lost my balance. I pulled my head back and crouched precariously on my side of the boulder, releasing my breath as quietly as I could. I was trembling. By some miracle I had not made sufficient noise to attract his attention. He was unaware of my presence. Now what in the hell was I supposed to do? There he was, almost magically. After all my long hours of searching for him, he had come to me!

I raised my head again to take another look. He remained with his back to me, staring with great concentration at some aspect of the landscape on the other side of the little clearing. He was wearing an old battered derby, a white shirt with sleeves partly rolled up, and a loose-fitting black vest opened at the front. His trousers were covered with paint marks. An old jacket was thrown on the grass to one side, and an opened canvas bag with a wide shoulder strap lay nearby. He held a palette and several brushes in one hand; the other rested on his hip. In tones too low to understand, even as close as we were, I could hear him muttering to himself.

Several minutes passed before I realized that he had not moved. He only stared straight ahead. Finally, he reached for one of his brushes with his free hand, mixed some pigment on his palette, and placed a stroke of paint on his canvas. He drew back somewhat to view the effect of what he had just done. Then he gazed again across the clearing. By a peculiar quirk of fate I was doing something that was forbidden: I was watching Cézanne paint! I was doing what others far more deserving could never do only because he was totally unaware of my presence. I was violating his privacy, a condition he had always gone to enormous lengths to protect.

Several more minutes went by before he mixed more paint and placed another stroke of pigment in the painting. This time, however, he no sooner glanced at his handiwork than he half-turned and violently threw his paintbrush on the ground and screamed, "Shit!"

Now this so startled me that I did lose control. I slipped, scraping the rock under my foot, while I made an involuntary vocal sound, and my game was up. Cézanne wheeled around, his eyes wide and frightened, as he cried, "Who's there?" What could I do except raise myself up, stick my head through the foliage and, with what was probably a dumb grin on my face, greet him by name?

At the sight of me he gasped, lurched backward, knocked his easel over—sending his canvas flying—and almost fell himself. I tried to calm him and at the same time climb over the boulders and through the foliage that stood between us. I jumped down into the clearing, landing a few feet from him. My appearance at full length dumbfounded and enraged him all the more. He dropped his palette, threw up his arms, screamed at me to go away, and started backing away rapidly, swearing at me the whole time.

It was so awful, Maurice. It couldn't have been worse. I had caught him completely unaware, and then when I leaped down on him from out of the trees he panicked. I shouted Émile's name, his name, my name, but all to no avail. Everything I tried to say only made things worse or else came to naught because his own shouting prevented him from hearing me.

By now he had backed all the way across the little clearing and was shaking his fists and waving me off. I tried to pick up his canvas and easel, but this made him all the more agitated, so I left them lying on the ground where they had fallen. Then I started to panic myself. I tried once more to tell him who I was and that I knew Émile Bernard, but none of this seemed to matter. He just kept waving his arms and shouting at me to go away.

In desperation, I tried thinking of names of other people who were his friends and with whom I was an acquaintance, however slight. I said that I knew Renoir and Monet, which was true, and that I knew Paul Gauguin, which was not. When he heard Gauguin's name, his eyes popped wider than ever, and he shouted, "Aha, just like him, you have come to spy on me. You want to steal my sensations, too. Never!"

At that, he turned and walked into the woods, stopping only after he had gone behind some tall bushes. He evidently thought that he was not visible to me, but I could still see the top of his derby. I knew he was standing there waiting for me to go away.

By now I was desolate. It had all been so badly bungled. This eccentric man was impossible, and I saw there was nothing more to be done to reach out to him. Before leaving, I set up his easel again, placing the canvas back on its holders. I leaned the palette against one of the legs of the tripod. Of course the palette had fallen face downward, dirt and pine needles mixing with the pigment. It was a mess. He was still standing behind the bush when I turned to go. I called to him that I was sorry to have disturbed him so. I told him I hoped that we might meet someday under more pleasant, less stressful circumstances. He neither moved nor answered.

I started off in the direction from which I had come. I circled around the boulders over which I had so recklessly climbed a few minutes before and, after walking a little distance in the direction of Aix, I paused. My frustration and embarrassment were most acute. The whole situation had gotten out of hand, and I felt myself as much the victim as the perpetrator of this fiasco.

Somehow I got it into my head to go back to the clearing to see what he would do. Oh, I had no idea of trying to approach him again; that would have been futile. I just wanted to watch him for a while without him seeing me. I came in sight of the clearing again but from a different angle, well protected by foliage. At first I could not see him where he was standing, but I had a good view of the easel and the painting, which remained as I had left them.

I crouched and waited behind a tree. Several minutes passed, and he did not appear. I wondered if he had just gone away, leaving everything behind, but that seemed absurd. Several more minutes passed without sight or sound of him. Then, when I was about to step forth myself, I heard a twig crack. I quickly ducked down, and in the next moment there he was, stepping forward at first cautiously and then more boldly. No sooner was he satisfied that he was alone than he started talking to himself. He went up to the easel and began examining the painting. When he took up the palette and found the mess that had befallen his paints, his body visibly stiffened and he cursed again. Then he cast around looking for his brushes, something I had not done when I hastily reassembled his things. He gathered up several of the brushes nearest him, looked closely at their tips, cursed again, and threw them back down on the ground.

Looking back at his canvas, he grabbed it with one hand, studied it for a moment at arm's length, and then, with a sweeping motion of his arm, flung it across the clearing. It sailed in a graceful arc and landed awkwardly in a bush ten yards from where he stood. From the moment it left his hand, Cézanne did not pay the least attention to its fate. He turned immediately to closing up his easel and storing away his palette and paints. In less than five minutes he was all packed, and without so much as a glance around him, he strode off in the same direction from which I had come, the route back toward Aix.

I did not move until I was sure he was well out of sight and hearing. When I felt confident that he must be gone, I went out into the clearing, going immediately over to the discarded canvas that lay wedged grotesquely between some branches of the bush where it had landed. I gingerly extricated it, finding to my amazement that it was unharmed. There were no tears or punctures, and even the paint was hardly smeared. This surprised me until I realized that most of the pigment was dry. This was a work he had begun at some earlier time and that he intended to continue today until yours truly sprang upon him.

But why should he have thrown the work away? It was quite advanced; he had obviously spent a great deal of time bringing it to its present state. Of course I knew immediately what I had to do. I brought it back with me; it's here now in my hotel room, and tomorrow, before I leave, I will arrange to have it delivered to his address in the Rue Boulegon.

It is a small vertical canvas. The image is made up of four stately pine trees, one of them very young and slender. The sapling stands gracefully between the two larger, left-hand trees. The straight, bare tree trunks divide the surface into a series of magnificently adjusted vertical spaces, each animated by a delicate play of arching branches and foliage. The green screen of pine needles is penetrated generously by blue sky, the whole worked out in a wonderfully rhythmic set of movements expressed through a tight network of closely knit brushstrokes. Three large rocks that ascend in a diagonal movement from lower right to upper left fill the bottom third of the composition. A tiny segment of horizon is visible in a narrow gap between the boulders in the middle of the picture, expressing in the most subtle way the presence of the horizontal. This tiny element anchors the strong vertical movements supplied by the tree trunks. The color tonalities are superb, consisting of purplish blues and acidy greens.

Answer me this, Maurice: how do you reconcile this serene and majestic conception with the strangely frightened and neurotic man who painted it?

Well, my old friend, there is little left to set down here about the events of this extraordinary day. No one, after all, can deny that I met Cézanne, though had I foreseen the circumstances of that meeting, I should have done anything to avoid it. Now what is to be done? Not even Émile's efforts to intercede on my behalf can make a difference at this point, I'm afraid. In fact, I hope my actions today do not somehow come back to sour Émile's relationship with him. Don't forget that I spoke Émile's name loudly and clearly. Cézanne must have heard it, whether or not he acknowledged it to me.

I need hardly say that I arrived back in Aix too late to catch my train, and, I might add, too tired and despondent to care. Only by writing this absurdly long letter have things fallen into a more benign perspective for me. I will always regret the encounter with Cézanne and can only console myself that I meant no harm. What most saddens me, I think, is that to him I am now just one more in that large and hostile crowd that threatens and rejects him. The irony is almost too much, since all I wanted to do was express my admiration and support of him. Surely the loss is far greater on my side than his. Meanwhile, what a great story, eh? I hope you have enjoyed it.

I managed last night to get a telegram off to my contacts in Avignon, telling them that I will arrive later today. I'm sure that no harm has been done on that score. Meanwhile, take care of yourself and greet the others for me. I'll see you very soon. Share this letter with whomever you wish, Émile included. What can it matter now?

À bientôt,
André

9

Brief but Firm

Thursday

Mr. Émile Bernard
Rue _____, Paris

Dear Sir,
    Inviting persons to intrude upon my privacy who are both unannounced and unknown to me is only calculated to arouse my displeasure.

Yours, etc.
P. Cézanne

10

LUNCHEON ON THE ROCKS

THE SIX OF THEM HAD BEEN WALKING for nearly an hour when Nicole paused at the side of the road. "Let's sit over there on those rocks and eat our lunch," she said. "The shade from those lovely old trees is perfect. And look, we can see the water as well as the chateau."

The water was that of the Yvette, a tiny tributary of the Seine by way of the Orge River; the chateau on the distant hill was La Madeleine, a ruin now but which in its heyday had ruled over the Chevreuse Valley southwest of Paris for a variety of aristocratic and kingly tenants, including Francis I. Now the area was easily accessible by train from Paris and had become a favorite place for Parisians to picnic.

Nicole called out again. "This way, everybody. I'm starved."

She ran in the direction she had pointed. The great stones were piled up like steps, and Nicole nimbly climbed to the highest one, where she gracefully perched herself to watch the others slowly walk toward her. No one in the group protested or even hesitated; all turned in compliance with her command, glad that someone else had made the choice. Maurice and Roger, who had fallen some distance behind the others, hardly looked up as they turned and headed toward the rocks, their conversation not missing a syllable.

"It's what I think of as his drawing, Roger. Can't you see that? It's Manet's drawing. That's where he took his most radical steps, and that's what most inspired Cézanne."

"No, you make too much of that," replied Roger. "I can't agree. You simply go too far."

"Wait, hear me out."

Maurice took off his jacket and folded it over his arm. Next he pulled down his tie and opened his shirt collar. Roger sensed Maurice's excitement. He knew he was in for one of his friend's harangues. "I'm thinking especially of Manet's paintings of the '60s," Maurice continued. "To me, they were his most daring works. In fact, in a certain sense, I think he backed away in his later years from the most radical implications of those earlier paintings. In a way, I think Manet lost his nerve…"

"Maurice, you're astounding," interrupted Roger. "Where do you get such outrageous ideas? The painter of *A Bar at the Folies Bergère* and *Rue Mosnier* lost his nerve? Ridiculous!"

"No. Wait. Listen to me."

Roger picked up his pace and walked ahead of Maurice. For him the discussion was not worth continuing. Maurice caught up with him.

"Listen, of course the *Bar* is a great painting. But think of his lady bullfighter. Think of *Victorine Meurand as an Espada*. You've seen that amazing painting; you must know it by heart too. He showed it in the Salon des Refusés. Remember? Along with his *Luncheon on the Grass*."

"Remember? I wasn't even born in 1863, and neither were you!" Maurice's allusion to that distant event made Roger grow peevish.

"Never mind," answered Maurice sternly. "I know all about that Salon. I've talked to people who were there. I've read accounts of it, and I've seen Manet's paintings. Believe me, I know what I'm talking about. The *Luncheon* brought the critics and everybody else down on him. A huge scandal for all the wrong reasons, of course, and the fools never even noticed that his *Espada* was by far the more revolutionary painting. Victorine dressed as a neophyte bullfighter, standing full length in the center of the canvas, dressed in that gorgeous black costume. Her red cape bunched up in one hand, her sword uplifted in the other."

Maurice turned his body to the side, raised his right arm as if about to thrust the sword upward and with his left hand dangled his rumpled jacket as if it were Victorine's cape. Roger could barely stop himself from exploding in laughter. Ignoring Roger's broad smile, Maurice went on in great seriousness. "But behind her, crowded into the upper right corner of the picture, were these diminutive figures of the picador on horseback taunting the bull and a small crowd of bystanders watching him."

Maurice bent over, making a horizontal gesture with his open hand at the level of his knees to indicate the small size of these background figures. "Do you see what I'm getting at, Roger? It's the scale. It's a matter of the scale between the foreground figure and those behind her. The realism is all wrong. Dramatically wrong. Victorine is much too big; why, by comparison to the others in the same picture space, she's a colossus. All the others, the bull and the horse included, are much too small. They're dwarves. No, smaller than dwarves."

Maurice searched Roger's face for signs that he understood, but his friend, shaking his head, only looked quizzically back at him. Maurice tried again. "But if it's all wrong as a realistic image; in truth, it's right as a revolutionary new painting, don't you see that? It's a conscious attack by Manet against a basic tenet of realistic painting. There's just no other way to look at it, Roger. He deliberately shattered the natural scale by painting in the same picture space two orders of figures that can't relate to each other in a realist system. That's what's so strange and exciting about this painting. In one stupendous effort—in a single work—Manet dismantled 400 years of realist painting!"

In the course of this exchange, the two young men had stopped walking. They stood facing each other, and Maurice had taken hold of Roger's arm to prevent him from walking off again. But with Maurice's concluding statement, Roger abruptly pulled his arm back. "How you rave! Maurice, sometimes your rants are amusing, even interesting, but at other times, like now, they are just ridiculous. Are you really trying to tell me that realistic painting has been all undone by a single canvas of Manet's?"

Maurice smiled for a moment as the absurdity of his own assertion came home to him, but then he immediately grew serious again. "Well, at least he put a big crack in the window. In that one painting, Manet broke with conventional visual representation in the most emphatic way. After that picture, painting no longer had to be a window on the world in the strictest sense. By willfully altering and mixing the scale of the figures that way, he took back the picture plane from its servitude to a rigid, outworn system of realism. He broke classical perspective in two with the same daring that Alexander cut the Gordian knot!"

"Damn it, Maurice, there you go again! It's always the farthest place out on the limb with you. You're so far out there I can't even be angry with you. The idea is just beyond believing." Laughing, Roger went on. "Can't you ever take a reasonable position? Does Manet need to assume such heroic stature?

Just like Alexander the Great, yet! And if Manet really did this extraordinary thing in his *Espada* painting, what did he lose his nerve about?"

Roger said this to his excitable friend without malice. He was used to Maurice's verbal extravagances, and today he felt like giving him free rein, though his desire to be generous was being tested by Maurice's excesses. Maurice's conceits could sometimes irritate him for days. At this moment he wanted to avoid that.

"He never followed through," said Maurice soberly. "Manet rarely took up this issue of scale again, at least never with the same force. His body of work lacks sufficient development on this theme to say he really carried the idea through. It's too bad. His reputation would be even greater today had he done so."

"Relax, old friend, I assure you his fame rests secure," said Roger with a broad smile.

"Yes, yes, I know. But the break with scale should head the list of the things he did," protested Maurice. "It was the most daring of all and had the profoundest implications. It was a revolutionary departure from the old way of seeing."

"Nonsense, Maurice. Your theory hangs by a thread. By your own admission the examples are so few. What if he never viewed what he did in any of the terms you describe? What if he was not assaulting Renaissance perspective at all?"

"He was!" interrupted Maurice hotly. "He did; he most assuredly did. It's plainly there in the painting for anyone to see. What he did is unmistakably…"

"And I suppose your argument goes on that Cézanne saw it all just as you do," Roger interrupted with enough sarcasm in his voice for Maurice to notice. "I suppose Cézanne has taken up Manet's cause. That's what you're driving at, isn't it? Come on, admit it." Now Roger was starting to perspire. Against his better judgment, he was becoming emotionally aroused. He did not accept Maurice's argument and was feeling put upon by Maurice's intensity. He felt he had to stand up to his dogmatic friend.

"In a certain respect, yes, Cézanne is following Manet," replied Maurice. "But he's not doing so on that particular issue, not necessarily regarding the issue of scale. It's deeper and broader than that. Cézanne understands the freedom that Manet was instinctively groping for. He could see the shackles of the old system Manet was trying to break. He saw the immense baggage that weighed down upon painting, accrued from the decades and centuries before. And from Manet, Cézanne gained the strength to make his own attack. That's why Cézanne is Manet's most important heir."

Without answering, Roger now did walk away toward the others, who were setting out the picnic on a flat rock. Maurice did not immediately follow his friend but hung back with his hands stuffed into his pockets. Muttering to himself, he made a half-hearted attempt to tidy his clothing. Without really looking at what he was doing, he partially tucked in his shirt, shook out his jacket, and ran his hand through his hair.

André stepped forward to meet Roger, a bottle of wine in one hand and a glass in the other. Drawing his friend aside, André asked what had been going on between him and Maurice. "What have you two been nattering about so intensely? At one point it looked like Maurice was about to launch into a mazurka!"

"Ha! Didn't you notice?" asked Roger, feigning surprise. "That was Victorine Meurand posing as a bullfighter. Surely you saw that. I mean, how could you not know that? And if you looked closely, you would have seen a group of miniature people running around her, including, even, a tiny bull and a picador on a horse!"

"Roger, what are you talking about? You are not making any sense. What has Maurice been carrying on about this time to get you so wrought up?"

"He's at it again. Maybe worse than ever," said Roger, raising both arms and then dropping them helplessly at his side. "He's pontificating…theorizing…imagining beyond believing."

"Here, let me pour you some of this good red." André couldn't help smiling. "So what is it about Cézanne this time? What's he got him up to now? Reinventing painting again, I suppose."

"No, not quite. He did that last week. This time it's Manet."

"What?" teased André. "You don't mean he's given Cézanne's place over to Manet?"

"Hardly. But he's got Manet, in a single picture, taking apart 400 years of Renaissance art, which, he's convinced, changed the course of painting forever."

"Oh, just which painting is that?" asked André.

"You ask him yourself," replied Roger. "I don't want to go through it all again. It's too hot. It's too silly."

Now Maurice approached the group but did not come up to where André and Roger were standing. Instead, he walked over to the others, who were seated on the rocks in the shade of the trees.

"Maurice, come here," said Nicole. "Sit by Mario and me. Look at you. Your shirt hanging out, your hair uncombed. You've been arguing again with Roger; we saw you from here. It's Sunday. You should relax. Have some of this good Bayonne ham and a glass of wine. Rest your brain."

Maurice flung his jacket down and gracelessly lowered his large body to the ground.

"My brain is fine," he grumbled. "It's others who have the problems understanding what are perfectly clear observations and ideas. It's really irritating. I make the most plausible statements and..."

"Oh, come on, Maurice," interrupted Mario, "stop complaining. Look. What a great day it is."

"He's right," chimed in Alain. "And look over there. What a view, eh? What do you think your Cézanne would do with that for a subject?"

Alain had pointed to a grassy place edged with bushes, behind which the waters of the little stream glistened. In the distance rose the hill and the castle. Maurice glanced in the direction indicated, and then with a wave of his hand he dismissed it.

"It's too pretty; it doesn't have his sense of structure," he said flatly. "Perhaps Renoir or possibly even Monet, but Cézanne wouldn't be bothered."

"Well, listen to that," laughed Alain. "He's right inside Cézanne's head now! Maurice, my friend, you've reached either new heights of clairvoyance or arrogance. All right then, how about over there?" Alain pointed in the direction of a group of closely spaced trees on the side of a sloping piece of ground. A farmhouse stood at the top of the rise to the right, and a narrow road angled up the slope toward it. Another group of trees on the left moved diagonally away in a line from the place where they sat. "Would that view be worthy of your Cézanne?"

Maurice's eyes followed the direction of Alain's pointing hand. He perused the site for a few seconds and then replied offhand, "Well, that's better than the other one, but he wouldn't paint it from here; he'd stand over there where his view would be perpendicular to the row of trees on the left."

Often, even more than the things Maurice said, it was the unequivocal assuredness of the way he said them that most exasperated his friends. Now it was Mario's turn to be irritated.

"Dammit, Maurice, how can you say that? I mean how can you say that with such certainty? Why couldn't he stand here and paint that scene? Of course he could! It's absurd to say he couldn't."

"I didn't say he couldn't," replied Maurice. "It's just my opinion that he wouldn't, that's all. Of course he could paint Alain's scene from here. They all could. Anyone could. But far more interesting, in my judgment, is whether he would."

"Well, can you beat that?" said Mario.

"No, wait," said Nicole, speaking up suddenly. "Let him explain. Go on, Maurice, why do you think he'd stand over there instead of here?"

Roger and André had now joined the group. Putting aside his anger over the discussion about Manet, Roger now found his friend's latest remarks interesting and spoke up before Maurice could gather himself to answer. "You know, Maurice has a point. Regardless of whether he's right about the precise place Cézanne would choose, the fact that a choice would be made is fundamental and undeniable. And that choice would have a lot to do with temperament and a conception of painting. Think of them all coming here. Let's say Cézanne or anyone else you care to name—Monet, Renoir, Pissarro, van Gogh, it doesn't matter. Of course, they could all paint any view we might choose. And they would each turn it into their own. After all, what else could Cézanne paint but a Cézanne? Or van Gogh a van Gogh? But left to their own devices and their own choosing, they surely would fan out in different directions, finding the views and the angles best suited to their personalities and their own particular vision. I think that's what Maurice means: nature, at least for a mature artist, is not an indifferent subject to be painted willy-nilly but a thing that in its choice embodies a great deal of the artist who chooses it."

As Roger talked, the others, with the exception of Maurice, looked around wondering what patch of landscape around them might attract one of the painters Roger had just named.

Then Maurice, who as they all knew always had to have the last word, spoke up.

"It's all of that and more, Roger. The choice embodies the culture and the whole history of art in the culture."

"All right, all right," cried Mario. "So what does our genius friend here think Cézanne would choose? What particular place around us here does Maurice think our great painter would select? Will he deign to share with us his special knowledge of the master?"

Mario's sarcasm brought smiles from the others, who all turned toward Maurice.

"You're on the spot now," André said to Maurice

Maurice lumbered to his feet and stood looking around him. Everyone waited silently.

"Frankly, I don't think he'd work here at all," he finally pronounced. "This is not his kind of countryside."

Maurice continued to look around. "No, he'd definitely go somewhere else. This wouldn't do."

At this, one voice rose testily. "Oh, c'mon, Maurice, you can do better than that! You're ducking the issue. Surely you can find a little something here that he might like to paint?" It was Mario again challenging Maurice and, as he spoke, he made a broad gesture encompassing all of the surrounding countryside.

"Surely there's some little thing here somewhere!"

"Mario's right," said André. "You can't get off that easily. If you are going to put down everybody else, then at least put your own choice on the line."

There were nods and sounds of agreement. Maurice smiled and looked around once more. He moved off from the group, slowly walking away ten or fifteen paces, his back to the others. Pausing, he turned and faced his friends as they continued to watch him. He stared in their direction for a moment or two and finally spoke. "I think he could be attracted to just that bit there where you are all standing. Yes, quite possibly something there."

Everyone turned in surprise and started backing away from where they had just been sitting and standing. Looming up before them was the great pile of boulders that had attracted them in the first place.

Maurice went on. "For choice, he might set himself up here where the planes of the rocks would most emphatically cross his line of sight. It seems to me that this position would give him the strongest sense of breadth across the base of his canvas."

Mario was still smarting from the earlier exchange and was not about to be persuaded here. "Oh, c'mon, Maurice. This is pure bluff. You don't know any more than I do about what Cézanne might choose for his motif."

"Hold on, Mario," said Maurice quickly. "Who said anything about his motif? That's a very deep and personal matter between him and his subject. I make no pretense to name his motif here. I am talking much more in general terms. I'm talking about the kind of subject matter he seems to prefer. There may be dozens of places like this where he might pause, attracted by the general character of the site, but yet not find a motif."

At this point Roger spoke up again in defense of his friend. "I hope you'll concede, Mario, that an artist does develop tendencies? This is what I think Maurice means. The direction of anyone's art is always toward a certain set of preferred forms and the problems that evolve from those forms. Maurice is just speculating, of course, but his basis for doing so seems legitimate to me."

"How simple you make it seem," persisted Mario. "You line this up, you line that up, and you think you have a Cézanne!"

For a moment no one spoke, until finally André ventured a remark that he hoped would settle matters. "Well, everyone, we'll all have a chance to see for ourselves when Monsieur Vollard opens the doors of his gallery to us next week. There will be many Cézannes to delight in and argue about. We can even put Maurice's feet to the fire right in front of his paintings."

Everyone laughed and looked at Maurice, who returned their affability with a sober stare. "I won't be there when the show opens."

"Won't be there?" cried André in a startled voice. "Surely you are joking. You, of all people."

"I wish I were joking. It's hard for me to believe too." With a wan smile, Maurice looked at each of his friends. "I've got to return immediately to my village, Arthez d'Asson, to be with my mother, who has had a serious accident. She has fallen and broken her hip. I received a telegram this morning from my sister in Pau; she wants me there as soon as possible. I leave by train for Bordeaux in the morning. I should have gone today, but I must wait until tomorrow to get the money I need."

"Oh, we're so sorry, Maurice," said André, putting an arm on his friend's shoulder. "Is there anything we can do?"

"Yes," added Roger. "You must tell us if there is anything

we can do."

"Thank you, but no, there's nothing, unless…" Maurice paused, and everyone waited in silence. "Except if one of you could write to me about the opening…about the work."

"I'll do it," said André eagerly. "Don't worry about that; I'll write you everything. You'll hear all about Cézanne's opening from me."

"Yes," seconded Roger. "Don't worry about that. We'll all contribute. We'll all see to it that André writes to you."

"How long do you think you will be away, Maurice?" asked Alain. "You'll be back before the exhibition finishes, won't you?"

"I can't say. I won't know until I get home. Yes, I hope I can return before the show closes. But my mother and my sister need me now, and I must think of them first."

"Well, what really bad luck, for your mother first of all, of course, but also for you," said Nicole, who came up to Maurice and took him by the arm. "Look, the afternoon is getting on. Let's sit here together and enjoy our picnic. Then let's walk to the chateau. No more arguments about art today. Let's give Maurice a pleasant day to remember when he is back home."

Everyone agreed and gathered around their friend.

11

RUE LAFFITTE

[Author's note: What follows are four letters written by André from Paris to Maurice at his home in the Pyrenees village of Arthez d'Asson. The chief subject of the letters concerns the exhibition of paintings by Paul Cézanne at the gallery of Ambroise Vollard that opened in November 1895]

November 12
Paris

Mon cher Maurice,

You won't be surprised to learn that ever since Monsieur Vollard swung open the doors of his gallery to let the world behold his Cézannes, there has been controversy. Exclamations of awe and pleasure vie with cries of anger and dismay. If it's not his color, then it's his drawing that galvanizes opinions. Amazement is shared on both sides. People are sufficiently moved for or against his art that perfect strangers talk to each other. I've even seen some people talking to themselves!

The master from Aix really does puncture most expectations about what a painting is, leaving little room for neutrality or indifference. Even his admirers exhibit surprise at what they see, confirming again how little his work is known. I saw Renoir, gesticulating wildly, grab Pissarro and pull him in front of a landscape, pointing to this and that. Oh, you should be here, Maurice!

But before discussing further what is currently on the walls and easels of the gallery in the Rue Laffitte, let me tell you about our preparations for the big event. On the night before the exhibition opened—two days ago now—Roger, Alain, Mario, and I had dinner together at my apartment. Into the wee hours we talked and smoked and drank far more than we should have, either worrying ourselves to death or else indulging in the most ridiculous fantasies. Of the latter, for example, we raised an image of the exhibition vindicating in a single blow all the wrongs the poor man has suffered...as if his art, once seen in abundance, would right everything—eyes immediately opening, opinions changing, the world getting the news, etc. Well, of course, it was all in fun; we didn't believe for an instant that such things would occur. But think of it: old Bouguereau astonished, falling to his knees in awe and gratitude; the next day he nominates Cézanne to the Academy. Hah!

Anyway, when I came down to the street the next morning, my head throbbed, and a cold wind added no relief. You would be surprised how much the weather has changed since you left. Summer has gone in search of some warmer place. But coffee and something to eat began to put me right, and soon I was off on some errands, after which I went to meet Alain and Roger at our usual place.

On the first day, we decided not to go to the gallery until late in the afternoon, so even after a long, leisurely lunch we still had time to kill. Feeling restless and excited, we decided to climb to the top of Montmartre in spite of the chill in the air. As we ascended Rue LePic, we passed number 54 where van Gogh once had lived with his brother. It was very touching to pause in front of that building, especially on such a day when Cézanne opened his first exhibition. Here he was, finally getting a chance so late in life at some recognition, an opportunity that Vincent, in his short life, never had.

We proceeded up the hill, the three of us mostly lost in our own thoughts. We stood for a long time looking out over the city. You know how everything appears from up there; even on sunny days, the impression is one of gray, the rooftops uniformly the same height and set so close together. There are just a few isolated forms that rise above that flat geometry: the towers of Notre Dame and St. Sulpice, the domes of the Invalides, the Panthéon, and the Val de Grâce. The Eiffel Tower and the Arc de Triomphe, of course, and just a few others. Not much gets above that implacable skyline. The heavy gray cloud cover made everything look even harder and colder than usual, more bleak and distant.

At one point Roger pitched a stone down a steep, empty part of the hill. As he lofted it, the space and distance just ate it up. It disappeared, landing somewhere below, out of sight and hearing, quite unnoticed. It made me think how hard it is to attract attention in this vast, gray city that swallows up just about anything that enters it. The construction of something that can rise above that uniform mass of tightly packed buildings—and the people who live and work in them—must be something very special.

And now, starting that day, our much-admired Cézanne would try his hand. Could he break through? Would he get the attention of this tough city that rewards so few and ignores and buries so many? When we descended back into the city, thoroughly chilled and shivering, we were, I think, a little less buoyant, a little less sure of ourselves.

But wait, I'm supposed to be cheering you up. And what better way than by whisking you off directly to the exhibition! My friend, how can I describe my feelings upon first entering that little gallery? Especially after all the buildup in our minds during these past weeks since we first heard about the exhibition. Think of it: paintings crammed everywhere, and they were all Cézannes! Maybe forty or fifty of them visible at once, almost cheek by jowl. There were landscapes, portraits, bathers, still lifes all set indifferently, side by side. And there were others stacked up, many more than Vollard could display at one time. Somebody said Cézanne had sent 150 pictures.

At first I couldn't concentrate on anything. My eyes darted recklessly from one canvas to the next, hardly pausing to take in more than its minimal identity as a landscape, a still life, or a figure composition. Colors blended into one gorgeous blur. Apples, flowers, drapery, faces, trees, rocks; it was as if my eyes, in defiance of what was possible, attempted to see everything at once! Only when Roger came up to me, caught my arm, and dragged me to one side to view a particular painting did I finally collect myself enough to take in a single canvas with some care. And what a beauty it was!

To the right was a huge face of rock composed of the most intense burnt-reds and oranges. In the left half of the composition was a path in similar tones surrounded by gorgeous greenery rising up in tiers and capped by the bluest of blue skies. It was the rock quarry at Bibémus, it just had to be! I'm sure of it, and how well I should know, right? That color is unmistakable. Roger, who was every bit as excited as I was, kept pointing to the main contours in the painting and muttering something about "the cohesion of the planes."

My eyes strayed, almost without my consent, this time settling on a still life. What charm and mystery, Maurice!

Strange, inexplicable spaces and angles were everywhere. The painting was dominated by a marvelously decorated blue drapery crawling with a sinuous floral design. Nestled carefully among the oval folds were various pieces of fruit, a wine bottle, a carafe, and a drinking glass. Everything was somehow flattened out, the space itself compressed. Most astonishing of all was the way the contours of the wine bottle and the carafe were distorted. Imagine, actually violating the clear and precise symmetry of a geometrically formed object! In terms of conventional seeing, the contours of this glass decanter looked very strange, but its relationship to the drapery was dancelike. And all of this set against an austere wall divided into a few simple vertical and horizontal sections brushed in a variety of subdued blues. It was as if this painted world were a fluid, insubstantial thing following the laws of some unearthly physics.

Another still life that captivated me was composed of a large round basket of apples in one corner, tipped forward toward the viewer. Other apples that might have spilled out of the basket swarmed across and beyond the ruts and gullies of a piled-up piece of drapery. At the rear of the table and to the right stood a dish of stacked-up lady fingers, and a wine bottle leaned up against the basket, seeming to watch over the proceeding like a spectator! No, I'm being silly, except the painting conveyed such a sense of gay and riotous move-ment and precarious balance.

The cloth was painted in an extraordinary number of col-ors—blues through pale greens and light mauves—yet it still communicated a distinct sense of white. It was a reprise of the porcelain sugar bowl and dish that Roger was so taken by in the still life we saw at Tanguy's this summer. Vollard told us later that the painting was just one of a very few that Cézanne had ever signed, testifying to one of the rare times when he was satisfied.

And believe it or not, I saw both of the works at Vollard's that I had seen in Aix: the landscape with the mill wheel at the Château Noir and the patch of forest he was painting when I came upon him in the quarry! Yes, the very one he threw away and that I retrieved and sent back to him. Just the sight of that picture made me shiver. That awful encounter still haunts me.

A great to-do is being made of many works that contain little open spaces of unpainted canvas. These paintings are unfinished, but strangely it doesn't seem to matter. It's a most astonishing thing, Maurice. Everyone is commenting about this. Silly as it sounds, these "unfinished" works convey a perfect sense of completeness! It's hard to explain, though I don't doubt that you have observed this and have a theory of your own.

Roger thinks it has something to do with Cézanne's procedure. For him, nothing exists in isolation; everything presents itself to him in context. Any form, color, or tone requires support by the forms or colors that surround it. Only then does any part have a meaningful place. This requirement tends to make Cézanne continuously paint all over his canvas, bringing along, as far as possible, everything at once. The result is that wherever he stops, there is always an overall sense of completeness to that point. His art, in large measure, is a slow pulling together of numerous parts, and as he has been known to say, linking these elements together into a seamless whole is a trying and most difficult challenge for him.

I did not see any of Cézanne's own colleagues on that first day, though I'm sure Pissarro, Monet, and the others will be coming along soon enough. I talked with Monsieur Vollard briefly. He seemed pretty tense, watching closely everyone's reaction to the work. I'm sure he feels as if he is out on the edge. He must expect the possibility of considerable controversy. He said he has no idea whether Cézanne will come to Paris to see his own show. When I mentioned the small banquet we hoped to give in his honor, Vollard shook his head and said, "Don't count on it." But I still can't believe he won't come. He must. His deliberately not coming seems ridiculous.

Well, my friend, it's late and I'm tired. There're so many more things to talk about, but these must wait for other letters. I'll try to get the next one off to you in a few days. The exhibition raises so many questions and excites so much wonder. Most of us are still just getting a feel for what Monsieur Vollard has arranged for us to see. It will take many more visits for us to plunge very deeply into this man's extraordinary vision.

Know that you are sorely missed here, not only by me but all the others too. I can just imagine the arguments Cézanne's paintings will arouse between you and Roger, for instance. All send greetings to you and best wishes to your mother.

Á bientôt,
André

***

November 16th
Paris

Mon cher Maurice

When I went to Monsieur V's gallery this morning, he came up to me immediately with his latest tale about visitors to his exhibition. It seems that late yesterday afternoon two men came in, one of whom was blind. From the way the two men related to one another, it was soon clear to Vollard that the potential client was not the man who could see but the man who could not. The other gentleman was his friend who had come along to help him get around and to describe the work. They went through a number of paintings, the one describing the subjects and helping the other run his fingers over the painting surfaces. Finally a choice was made, a landscape done with a palette knife. The blind man confided to Vollard that although his passion turned more toward drawing, he didn't mind from time to time purchasing a work that had a hardiness of execution! And then the payoff: he really didn't know anything about Cézanne or have any particular feeling for his work. What he did know was that Zola, whom he admired immensely, had bestowed his friendship upon the painter, and that's why he wanted the painting, as a kind of tribute to the writer!

I don't recall mentioning in my last letter that Monsieur Vollard has placed three of his Cézannes in a window facing the street, all nudes. And what nudes! Included is a *Leda and the Swan*. This painting is most strange and mystifying, and you must admire Vollard's nerve. As you can imagine, some passers-by are aghast, good taste and morals all ruffled. The same subject in the Louvre would not get them to raise an eyebrow, but here in the street, with the image so forcefully painted, arouses any amount of indignation. One of the newspapers has expressed in the most sardonic terms an anxiety that its female readers might become ill if they pass the window at 39 Rue Laffitte. Even Vollard's maid has felt the need to scold him about placing these works in the window.

So, to no one's surprise, the atmosphere in Vollard's little gallery is heating up. The complications and the eccentricities of the master's paintings are making the temperature rise. One comes by, according to Vollard, either to see the art or to see the "monstrosities." Make your own choice; there appears to be no middle ground.

Once when Roger and I arrived at Vollard's, two men who I'd never seen before were engaged in an out-and-out vilification of the paintings. They were so full of themselves and expressed their opinions in such loud, assertive voices that I suspect they were pleased to be overheard by anyone within listening distance. It was all so predictable. The taller of the two was incensed by the drawing in some of Cézanne's still lifes and figure paintings. He did not conceal his disdain for what he called Cézanne's "infantile efforts to draw." He pointed to a still life in which the perspective appeared disjointed, as if seen differently in different parts of the picture space. It made absolutely no sense to him, and he instantly made the snap judgment that Cézanne's skill was utterly amateurish. There was no thought whatsoever that what Cézanne had done could possibly be conscious or deliberate; it was automatically assumed to be bad drawing. This idiot's mind was shut so tight; he summed it all up with a remark to the effect that his five-year-old nephew could do better.

Not to be outdone, his shorter companion countered with a belittling query of equal banality: "Perhaps this Monsieur Cézanne is afflicted by some obscure disease of the eyes?" Roger, of course, got his dander up immediately. He would have gone directly to engage the two men in earnest, but I pulled him back, telling him not to bother because it was a hopeless waste of time. He checked himself for a moment but then, turning his back on the two, spoke to me in a very loud voice, saying, "Isn't it interesting how some people have stones for brains and react to innovation and courage only with burning scorn and jeering laughter?"

The two men avoided looking at Roger. The short one simply urged his friend to leave: "Let's not waste another moment on this pathetic rubbish." They departed without another word. The whole episode, of course, was silly, but it certainly demonstrated what Cézanne is up against in some quarters.

Then another man and a woman entered the gallery almost immediately. They looked at the work for some time. At one point, she confided to the man that she was happy such work was selling in the galleries. Then she told Vollard that her son painted without any more regard for drawing than this artist here. She was glad, she said again, that there was a market for this type of work. Vollard rightly chose this moment to dampen her innocent enthusiasm by telling her that the artist hardly covered expenses for his paint and canvas and that he had been working for thirty-five years virtually without recompense. She went out the door very depressed, followed by her triumphant husband, who taunted her by saying, "Monsieur Cormon is always saying in his art class that good drawing is everything." Vollard has other stories that are equally depressing.

On the other hand, Monet, Pissarro, Renoir, and Degas have all been in and are very excited about the work. Pissarro is thrilled by what he calls its "temperament." Some of them have bought works outright, and others have tried to arrange trades. Even crusty old Degas has been conquered by the work.

Just yesterday when I went to the gallery, a rousing discussion broke out between Roger, Mario, and two strangers who happened into the gallery. I must say right off that these two unknown persons, neither of whom were artists, displayed a rare open-mindedness in the midst of considerable skepticism. To say the least, it was refreshing; one could wish for many others like them. Neither had ever seen paintings like these, but instead of the usual wholesale condemnation, they were filled with curiosity and questions. Clearly they fell on the side of a kind of instinctive sympathy for the work, however much confused and uncertain they may have felt. What is that ingredient of temperament, I wonder, that keeps the mind open and interested even when the issues at hand are beyond immediate comprehension?

Sometime later, after the two strangers had gone, Roger waxed eloquently over a couple of the paintings in the show. One of them was a landscape painting with Mont Sainte Victoire in the background and parts of some trees in the foreground. Some branches of the nearby trees playfully followed part of the contour of the distant mountain, in a subtle way seeming to link the two together.

As Roger put it, those trees and that distant mountain are "mute, blind, and immobile." Their communication with one another is a pure invention inside Cézanne's head. His eye, his brain, and the exact position of his body in the landscape are what enable these two distinct and indifferent aspects of nature to come together. It is his eyes that discover the relationship, and his canvas is the venue where the connection is expressed. It's solely through his imaginative act, as it surges forth into a setting that contains a thousand possibilities, that just that particular alliance between the tree limbs and the mountain is made. The aspect of those tree branches in precisely that relationship to the unique configuration of the mountain is not a regular or enduring part of their natures; it's an extension or projection of his. His mind is not only the conduit that makes the communication possible; it's the sole source of whatever meaning the relationship has. This is so crucial that if he moves a step to his right or left, the relationship between these two objects changes or perhaps even vanishes.

Just so Roger wouldn't think he carried the day, Mario

made the point that framing or setting off objects or persons with foliage or architectural devices was an old classical trick easy to find in the museums. We all had a laugh, but Roger stuck to his guns. He argued that in this painting the foliage and the mountain had "parity." It is precisely that relationship between them that is the subject of the painting. The one is not a foil for the other.

Then the conversation moved on to Cézanne's color. Roger again stepped up and summarized the main debate as he saw it. He noted first that there are those who think that Cézanne's color is everything—even that he constructs form with color. Evidently the master himself has given credence to this point of view, having said as much to Émile and others. But as Maurice Denis has said, what Cézanne says on Monday, he doesn't necessarily say on Tuesday. So there is another camp that claims his drawing is easily as important as his color.

The color camp says his color and drawing are so fused as to be one and the same. The others argue that he freely and often avails himself of pure line. They point to numerous instances when the forms are outlined or "drawn." No matter how tentative his lines may seem or how broken or segmented, what can only be called "lines" are there. And often they are depicted in colors—most frequently in blue—at variance with the local color of the forms they define. Even though Cézanne reiterated the truism that there are no lines in nature, it's undeniable that he availed himself of them. It's as if to say there may not be lines in nature, but there are in art.

On quite a different matter, there is much buzzing and speculation about whether Cézanne will come here to see his exhibition. No one knows anything for sure. I mentioned Vollard's skepticism in my last letter; even Cézanne's son

Paul doesn't know what his father will do. The banquet in his honor has not taken hold; Cézanne, as far as I know, has never even answered the written invitation sent to him by Pissarro or a follow-up by Renoir.

Well, it is of no great consequence whether that particular event happens or not. It occurs to me, however, that I should probably stay out of sight if such an event ever did take place. After my encounter with him at the rock quarry, can you imagine his reaction if he caught sight of me again! But as for him not seeing his own exhibition, that still seems to me to be ridiculous. I can't imagine how he could resist.

Maurice, I'm going to close this here. Until my next letter, I hope I have put together enough to satisfy your eager desire for news about this grand extravaganza of art in Paris! Oh, if it only were true! If only these blind Parisians would open their eyes to see the treasures on display in the Rue Laffitte. Maybe this will occur at some future time. Who knows?

I'm having dinner this evening with Roger, Nicole, and Alain. Be assured that I will pass along your regards. All of us earnestly wish that your mother's recovery is going forward with as much speed as possible. I will write again by the end of the week.

Ton ami,
André

***

November 21st

Mon cher Maurice,

The evidence at Vollard's of Cézanne's experiments with color is in wondrous abundance. And some of it is driven by more than instinct or taste or Pissarro's favorite term: *temperament*. Some of Cézanne's color is very reasoned and conceptualized. It's color that's made, not found.

I'm thinking particularly of a rather large canvas of a woman in full dress seated beside a plain table on which rest a coffee pot, a cup, and a saucer. The sitter is possibly Madame Brémond, Cézanne's housekeeper. But she sits with the dignity of a monarch enthroned, her strong hands resting in her lap. I remember Madame Brémond when I met her briefly in Aix, and much of what I remember about her is here in the painting. There is the same severity in the expression on her face, the tight folds of her hair, the cut of her long-sleeved dress, which is pleated in the upper part and firmly tied with a belt at her waist. In a fanlike shape, her skirt falls gracefully to the bottom of the canvas. The thin collar is buttoned tightly around her neck. All these strictures in the painting are worth mentioning because in their contrasts they seem to make more apparent the glorious and airy color of her dress, which is a commanding and most imperious blue.

Indeed, this is no ordinary blue, my friend. It's one that has been teased and tempted into extending itself even to its farthest blueness! It's a blue that has been pulled and stretched to its very limits, to where, if it dared another step, it would leave blue behind to join one of its neighbors in the color spectrum, either green or purple. In other words, this is not color that you or I are apt to run into by accident. This is not the reflected light of the Impressionists, either, though those theories and practices may have had some influence here. This color is purely Cézanne's invention; it is contrived by the application of optical logic combined with rudimentary color theory.

In certain places across her dress, especially in the area of the skirt, Cézanne infiltrates his blue with minute touches of red, moving the blue pigment gingerly and masterfully toward purple, and with the smallest amounts of yellow that permit the appearance of greenish tones. While the primacy of blue is never threatened, there are, however, these gorgeous passages of blue toward red and blue toward yellow, passing through, as it were, the whole gamut of blue, the whole thrilling life of blue! You must see this painting, Maurice. By God, someday it should be in the Louvre. Surely there is not another such blue in that whole barn of a museum, not even Fra Angelico's blue.

It is worth noting that while Cézanne attempts this sort of color elsewhere, he by no means does it everywhere. I found similar treatments in a couple of portraits of Madame Cézanne among the pieces in the show; the same goes for some landscapes and still lifes. It is clearly something that interests him and that he can do at will and with great subtlety. Perhaps it is analogous to a poet who can use one poetic form—say a sonnet—but then writes in other forms as well.

It is also interesting that he does not use this sort of "stretched color" throughout a single composition. The other parts of the painting of the lady seated beside the coffee pot are colored more along conventional Impressionistic lines. The tablecloth, for instance, is painted in yellows and reddish browns but not in anything approaching blue or green.

Roger has been to the gallery every day since it opened. He is beside himself with excitement and spends hours at a time there, as if he would memorize everything Cézanne has done. He must be driving Vollard crazy. He also seems to have made a new friend there, a poet, who shares similar enthusiasm for the work. He told me this person's name, but at the moment I can't recall it. He's either German or Austrian, and he is employed as Rodin's secretary.

Well, where to stop with all this chatter? Before I wear

you out, let me make one more observation about a fascinating aspect of some of the paintings. Certain attitudes about light in Cézanne's pictures have aroused our interest. In a number of them, especially certain still lifes, the light source has a strange, undeniable effect on the objects it falls across. Bottles, jars, and bowls tip or lean toward the light! Sometimes even doorways, wainscoting, tables, chairs, and bookcases seem to do the same thing. It is fascinating. In the case of fruit, the contours swell or grow more rounded on the lighted side. In contrast, the sides away from the light tend to flatten out or collapse.

I'm thinking of a still life in which a bench covered by the heavy folds of a printed blue cloth supports a ceramic olive jar, a round ginger pot, a large green melon, and a plate of apples. A rum bottle stands at the rear, and behind them all rises a small desk or stand against which leans a stalk bearing three small eggplants. It is a curious collection of things, to be sure, but even more unexpected is the way these objects respond to the light that enters from the left.

The contours of the melon and the ginger pot are distinctly fuller and more rounded on their sides toward the light. The shadowed sides are shallower. Even the distortion in the olive jar is more pronounced on the side that receives the direct light. Perhaps most surprising of all, the verticals in the background—a doorway, the little table, the rum bottle—also all bend in the direction of the light. Even the plate of apples is tipped to the left.

Once you notice this peculiar structuring of the forms, it becomes mesmerizing. Cézanne sets up a dynamic that exerts an organizing force throughout the painting. It's as if Cézanne's light shares some of the power of the moon that pulls and tugs at the tides of the oceans! And what is he expressing about the power of light to reveal form and the character of darkness to diminish it?

There are perhaps several ways of understanding all this, but certainly this idea of light pushing back darkness is one possibility. Light is the means by which the world becomes visible. The implied transformation from one state—darkness—into the other—light—is made explicit in the painting by endowing the objects with a physical expression of movement: things literally bending, leaning, or swelling toward the light.

We are in awe at what Cézanne will surrender for the sake of his concepts. The most common-sense visual relationships and conventions may be forsaken in order to achieve the desired effects. And, indeed, to say the things that he wants to say, what choice does he have? But how he has laid himself open to misunderstanding and censure. The accusations over the years that he cannot draw must be particularly galling. What I have just been trying to describe is best characterized as drawing. And what drawing!

A surprising number of other paintings here, including certain portraits, seem to follow the same scheme. The woman in blue seated beside the coffee pot is again a good example. Not only is the axis of her body leaning toward the light, so are all the vertical edges of the paneling behind her.

At the same time, the concept never becomes formulaic. As in the special working of color already noted, this concept of light is something Cézanne will avail himself of at certain times and not others. His willingness to experiment and to follow out the implications of his research is always subject to his own severe scrutiny and taken up by him only intermittently.

One thing we've more or less agreed upon is that Cézanne is not an Impressionist, at least not in the sense of portraying the momentary and the fleeting. His art has nothing to do with the weather or the effects of the weather or the movement of things stirred by the wind or the flow of water. Neither fog nor mist nor climate nor time of day matters in a canvas by him. To make him an Impressionist you'd need to redefine the movement as something to do with a new space and structure. And, yes, with the mechanisms of perception.

So what if none of what I've been writing to you is more than very tentative? Who knows the truth, eh? As if there really is a unique and perfect truth. Certainly the work is marvelously provocative; disputes about it spring forth like mushrooms after a rain. One thing is certain: to take in one of his paintings requires time and thought. His images are wells filled with sparkling ideas and sensations.

Maurice, these few letters to you seem so inadequate. There are many more issues here, and even the ones I have touched upon go so much deeper. Nothing can substitute for you seeing the works for yourself. As soon as you can return here, you will be astounded at what there is to see.

Ton Ami,
André

***

November 23rd

Dear Maurice,

I am leaving Paris in an hour for Chartres, where my aunt lives. I will have time while I am there to write you in full. I received your letter this morning; it must have crossed with another from me that I posted two days ago. The setback your mother has had saddens me. I realize now that your chances are slight for getting here to the Cézannes before the exhibition closes. At least know that there is no great rush in the world to buy Cézannes! Vollard will no doubt have plenty of them on hand whenever you do return.

I speak for all of us here in sending our best regards and fondest hopes for your mother's speedy recovery. I will write to you more at length tomorrow.

A handshake in friendship,

André

12

The Third Visitation

CÉZANNE HAD SET HIMSELF UP IN AN OPEN FIELD in front of a landscape rich in contrasts. The many greens of numerous trees vied with the siennas and ochers of the Provençal earth for dominance of the hillside. The artist filled his canvas from side to side with the bulk of the curving slope before him. Near the base of the hill, a farmhouse rose in the midst of a grove thick with dark green fir trees. The trees thinned out partway up the steep hill, permitting large patches of bare ground to appear. A single cypress tree broke above the curve of the ridge, penetrating the blue sky above.

The painter loaded his brush with an earth-green pigment altered by small quantities of burnt umber and Prussian blue. He raised his eyes for one more glance at his subject only to see, to his astonishment, a dark, shadowy form slowly disengage itself from the mass of shadows engulfing the nearest trees. The dark shape stepped toward the artist, turning his surprise to chagrin. In the bright sunlight the shadows vanished, revealing not only a man but, of all men, the one the artist had the least desire ever to see again.

"Ah, there you are, hard at work as usual," said the stranger cheerfully.

"You!" groaned Cézanne. "How did you find me this time?"

The stranger carried a small travel bag and approached the painter with a bright smile on his face. "Well, this is more like it," he said. "At least the ground is flat and there's room to move around. Thank heaven this is nothing like the first time we met when you made me climb that dreadful hill behind the Château Noir."

The stranger set his bag down and turned in several directions to take in the view.

"Here to lecture me again, no doubt," grumbled the artist. "Damn all, go find someone else to harass."

"Really, Cézanne, you're so unfair."

"But I don't know why you keep forcing yourself on me like this." Cézanne shook his fist. "You know I can't stand you. You know I don't want to talk to you. You're like some demon come to torment me. The first time was a nuisance, the last time an aggravation. Now you're becoming a definite pain in the..."

"Now who's judging? Who's lecturing?"

"Move out of the way. You're standing in front of my motif!"

The stranger calmly looked behind him at the hillside out of which he had just walked. Taking up his bag, he moved to one side. "Go on with your work. Don't mind me. I can't see what you are doing from here."

The artist cursed and turned back to his canvas.

"Well, they're certainly talking about you in Paris," began the stranger. "Your show is making quite a stir, at least in the little circle of your friends and acquaintances, and among others who happen to wander into Monsieur Vollard's gallery. The variety of opinions is extreme, but hearing that should not surprise you."

The artist did not answer or even look up from his painting. Opinions of any kind about his work, good or bad, always made him tense and uneasy. The stranger went on talking, seemingly unconcerned about whether the painter responded or not.

"I'll give you this much: the art you make is hard to ignore. Opinions fly like sparks. Your work draws out the best and the worst in those who see it. A thing you have painted is pronounced by this one as a 'masterpiece' and by the next one as a 'monstrosity.' It's fascinating how the same works can arouse so many contrary responses, don't you think? Is there anything on which people are more apt to disagree than art? Liking or not liking your paintings seems to be easy and popular. Remaining neutral is apparently impossible."

Cézanne continued to appear engrossed in his painting. He had already heard reports from various sources about the range of views his art was inspiring. Vollard had sent word of odd encounters with people who were stopping by his little gallery on the Rue Laffitte. There was a man who apparently made his wife, an amateur artist, look at the Cézannes as a kind of punishment.

As if he had been reading Cézanne's thoughts, the stranger added another anecdote. "Oh yes, and who do you suppose came by? None other than one of the pillars of the Academy, the great Gérôme himself! I'm sure you feel honored. As he looked at your paintings in the window, Vollard overheard him say in the most hostile tones to his companion, 'So they don't need to draw anymore, eh?' What do you say to that, my friend?"

"I drop my trousers to honor his opinion with my loudest fart!"

"Really, Cézanne, how vulgar! I saw him recently at a public function at the Academy. He and the others were dressed in full regalia. Quite an impressive sight. Medals galore. It seems to me that Gérôme has an infinitely better feel for the public taste than you do. He knows what they want, how to please them. You see, your art challenges the conventional expectations, while his confirms and pampers…"

"This is a line of conversation only calculated to enrage and depress me. Is this what you want?"

"No, of course not. You're right, lets drop it there," the stranger quickly replied.

"On the other hand, dear fellow, your friends and admirers troop to Vollard's to see your paintings, and their verdicts are highly favorable. What a pity the gallery is so small. He can only show part of your work at any one time. He's got stacks of canvases standing around."

Cézanne had gone back to studying his painting, making it unclear if he was still listening. Hearing praises of his work was never a likely way to capture his attention. Positive things said to him about his efforts were just as liable to raise his suspicions as would critical things. Distrust surrounded everything he heard about his work.

The stranger either did not notice the painter's apparent indifference, or he didn't care, and he went right on talking. "Pissarro, Renoir, Monet, and the others…Bernard, Signac, Denis…they're all pleased. Some of them are thrilled. Pissarro especially admires your still lifes. He spends hours there explaining and praising the strength and beauty of your art to anyone who will listen to him. It's almost as if he feels he has something personal at stake and seeks vindication for his unswerving support of your work. What a loyal friend, eh? But they all feel you're a worthy colleague who deserves much more respect than you've so far received. They regret the abuses you have had to endure in the past and hope this exhibition marks a turning point for the better in your fortunes. Really, Cézanne, their feelings are warm and admiring toward you. Even Degas is excited and purchased two of your works. Degas and Renoir were so charmed by one of your drawings of a bowl of fruit that they drew lots to see who would purchase it. Now, isn't that proof of support and admiration?"

The stranger stared at the artist in mild disgust tempered with sadness. He sensed the insecurities that held Cézanne prisoner. For so many years the artist had worked alone and outside the mainstream. The doubts that perpetually plagued him simply could not be cast off by a sudden wave of praise.

The stranger went on with his report from Paris. "You know, the mood and richness of your color has excited much attention. Practically everyone is in agreement on that score. The qualities that you evoke in your color are often stunning. Renoir was in ecstasy about several of your forest landscapes. There is less accord about your drawing, but even then many applaud what they call your 'gaucheries.'"

At that last comment, it was clear the artist was not totally indifferent to the stranger's speech. Cézanne looked up sharply and said, "What do they mean by my 'gaucheries?'"

"Yes, this is what I tried to protect you from," said the stranger. "But you wouldn't listen. You had to pursue this insane impulse to exhibit."

"But what are they calling my 'gaucheries'?" demanded the artist.

"Your clumsy distortions of form...but many like them," replied the stranger. "They like your awkwardnesses. They think they reveal your temperament...your individuality. They show us who you really are. Your anxieties. Your struggles. Take those broken lines, or multiple contours that describe the edges of tree trunks in some of your landscapes or the edges of some of the pieces of fruit or bottles in your still lifes. Well, your admirers feel these are signs of your uncompromising honesty…your humility before what, for you, are insurmountable obstacles. They see these tentative marks as your hesitations before the complexities of nature. These qualities, which you do not try to hide, make you seem more vulnerable…more human. They let us see your painfully careful explorations…your indecision… your difficulties."

With an angry cry, Cézanne stepped away from his easel. "And these are my friends? My admirers? The fools! Damn them all. They are blind. My anxieties? My hesitations? What rot! These are not the things I'm trying to express. This is not what my art is about. Can't they see? Why can't they see? It's a matter of my sensations. Everything I do in my paintings is meant to express what I see…the way I see. What they are calling my 'gaucheries' are deliberate. They are all carefully considered choices and decisions. All of them! These so-called 'gaucheries' are at the heart of my conceptions. The imbeciles!"

The artist's bitter words had a strong and immediate effect on the stranger, who now became angry also. He was incensed at Cézanne's unwillingness or inability to concede any difficulties in his painting. He drew close to the artist and in a tense and grating voice said, "You will allow that there are—what shall I call them?—certain eccentricities in your paintings? In the way you shape certain things…a cup here, a bottle there… maybe a tabletop…even a human head? The way you color them? The way you draw them? The way certain things lean and tip strangely? Edges that are discontinuous…broken? You will allow the truth of what I'm saying here, won't you? There are such peculiar ways you seem to see things. I mean, you appear to have abused certain conventions or at least stretched them to limits beyond easy recognition or understanding. Your use of perspective, for instance, just to name one. All in all, quite a special way of seeing."

"Poppycock!" snapped Cézanne, who was too angry to give in on any point. "I don't see anything in the subjects I paint that anyone else can't also see if they would only look and then think about what they see and how they see. You sound like all the rest of them."

"No, listen to me. You get into nuances of seeing that for the rest of us don't make any sense. You paint subtleties that are meaningless to most of us."

"No!" replied the painter. "My intention has always been to express myself as clearly and logically as I can."

"Well, damn it all, Cézanne, think about it. You seem to make the ordinary fact of seeing into…I don't know…some kind of ritual act, as if it were a miracle or something. Seeing is just seeing for the rest of us. Ah, but not for you. I've watched you sitting for hours in front of your damned apples, staring at them as if they were the most important things on earth, as if they contained some potency or essence of life itself. You seem to look at them in the way a blind man touches them. You don't see a luscious piece of fruit as Gérôme does or even as Renoir does…soft and sensuous to the eye and touch, full and round in space. Oh no, your apples are either as solid as granite, as if a sculptor had hacked them out of stone, or else they pulsate with some kind of inner life. How many apples have you painted by now? It must be crates full! And you paint them as if your life depended on it. You paint them as if they were the whole universe. You expect us to believe that apples are not only beautiful but important! I mean, think about it: nine reds in an apple. And then you wonder why people can't understand what you are getting at. What in God's name is so noble or inspiring about a silly apple?"

A pause.

These angry remarks by the stranger so caught Cézanne by surprise that he was unable to speak. For him, the apple was almost a sacred object. It was a metaphor for all nature. It contained within its tiny form a compressed version of all the issues of his art. Light, shadow, color, form in space, optics, and all the rest. If looked at properly, all was therein contained. Two or three of these little pieces of fruit set side by side, or overlapping one another, could, in the old artist's mind, offer up a lifetime of productive study. This little object could open the way into all the intricacies of the visual world. In certain very deep and private moments, Cézanne dreamed of making paintings of just these very objects, paintings that would astonish those who viewed them. Yet just how far away he was from achieving such a dream was made painfully clear by this ignorant man who demeaned and dismissed this glorious gift of nature, throwing it aside as if it were nothing.

The stranger's persistent nagging broke into the artist's reverie.

"Go on, tell me. What?" goaded the stranger.

Cézanne stared hard at the stranger but remained stubbornly silent.

"Aha, you can't tell me, can you? You are mute, I knew it."

Taking the artist's refusal to speak as a sign of acquiescence, the stranger plunged ahead. "What you are attempting is impossible. You seem to be trying for some odd beauty based on new and strange ideas. But you leave us bewildered, if not outraged. We have nothing to go on, nothing to compare your work to except what we already know, what we have been brought up with. What you paint isn't knowable to us yet. It is inexpressible. Your displacements, your deformations...what do they mean? Because we do not understand them, we are at a loss for words. We need a new descriptive language so that we can think about your images...talk about them!"

The stranger was excited now. Saying these things to Cézanne was important to him. He could not say why, but he was driven by some compulsion to speak these words.

"Most people don't really want new ideas," the stranger continued. "They talk about originality as if they approved of it and coveted it, but all they really want is confirmation of what they already know and believe. Truly new ideas carry with them responsibilities most of us don't want to bother with. For one thing, a new idea makes you rethink your position, makes you realign what you have grown comfortable with, maybe even makes you cast out some of your favorite verities."

The painter sat with his head down, his arms at his side, as if in resignation, waiting for his antagonist to finish. He looked neither at the stranger nor at his painting.

The stranger had not finished speaking his piece and knew that this was his last chance to say what he wanted to say.

"In your paintings, you seem to set aside what the rest of us have come to admire. Call them 'conventions' if you like, but they evolved over a long period of time and lead to what we consider to be beautiful and inspiring. And now you are after some new beauty...some new order...as if the old ways of representing things were no longer appropriate...no longer viable. Isn't the world changing enough? In art, at least, can't we preserve the old ways...the old values? Must everything change, disappear?"

Struck suddenly by his own reactionary point of view, the stranger laughed. "Listen to me. In art I'm the one who is conservative, while you are absurdly orthodox in everything except art!"

Cézanne looked up at the stranger for a moment, his face passive, his hand raised as if to say, "Enough, enough." But the stranger ignored the silent plea.

"If there is something of value in your art, it is beyond us so far. Mind you, I'm not saying there isn't something there. How would I know? I don't understand what you are trying to do, and most others don't either, even, as you say, your friends and admirers, all of whom you have just called fools. Your painting is a meditation on levels of experience to which the world is indifferent; most people need more time to digest it. You keep complaining about realizing your sensations, but how should the rest of us deal with that? Why should we care about your problems?"

Cézanne's face turned angry. He was reaching the limits of his tolerance for being harangued by his unrelenting critic.

"Oh, don't give me that nasty look," went on the stranger, his arrogance barely concealed. "And don't dismiss us as if we don't matter. Don't dismiss me! Like it or not, I am your audience. It's only people like me who are educated and interested. You are therefore essentially painting for me, for people like me."

The stranger pointed his forefinger vigorously at himself. "It's our sensibilities and intelligence you must address. If not us, who do you have? Who else will even look?"

The old artist recognized a certain truth in the words of the stranger. In one way or another, this verbose and preposterous man was addressing issues in his art, especially relating to the clarity of his ideas as expressed in the paintings themselves.

"Let me put it another way," continued the stranger. "You have devised some special encoding of your sensations that, to the rest of us, is mysterious and unknown. We have not broken your code, so the messages…the ideas or feelings that you have left behind in your paintings…remain largely meaningless to us. We look at your work with our old eyes and find elements that do not fit our vision or our understanding. You have focused for so long and with such patience and earnestness on the subtleties of seeing that you have left us far behind. For years, you have trained yourself to observe the world in certain ways that fall far outside of ordinary looking. And then you are enraged when we can't keep up with you."

Speaking slowly and with intensely measured restraint, as if to do otherwise would unleash great fury, Cézanne at last broke his silence. "I have never wanted to change art; I have only sought to add to it. My sole aim has been to present to the public my own interpretations of the spectacle of nature that surrounds me. I have always believed in the logical unfolding of what I see and feel before nature. It is my belief that with a concept of nature and a sufficient method to express it, one should achieve the means to make oneself intelligible to the public. If I have not yet done so—as the things you report to me make me believe— then so be it. I am too old now ever to hope to fully realize my conceptions, but as well as I can, I must go on. Talk is worthless; the work itself must prove me right."

And then in a sudden change of tone, the fierce old pride flashed forth. "I am the primitive of a new way!"

Cézanne stopped speaking as suddenly as he had begun. He turned back to his canvas and seemed to have no more to say. Nor did he seem to seek any response. The stranger stood silently as the artist reached for his palette and took up his brushes. The calm that seemed to have descended upon the painter caused the stranger to marvel at him once more.

"You know, Cézanne, in spite of myself, I like you. I even like what you paint. I don't understand it, of course, but there's something about what you do that attracts me. There's an intensity…a conviction…or maybe it's an obsessiveness that fascinates me. The press and the public have torn you apart for the way you paint, but you keep on. That's really commendable. I think it's also ultimately stupid, of course, as I've already told you, but still somehow remarkable. I admire your stubbornness and your persistence, regardless of the obstacles and the setbacks."

The painter was absorbed in his work and did not answer; it was not even clear to the stranger if he was listening any longer. "How different we are, Cézanne. It's as if all of these years you've been digging a hole deep and straight, while I have moved sideways through life making little more than a shallow furrow across a wide plain. I am curious about many things. I've dabbled here and there…a little of this, a little of that. You have chosen a single thing to do and nothing else. You are among that small group of adventurous and creative people who find a calling, who, through some odd and mysterious twist of your nature, have the capacity to throw yourself into a single pursuit and do it even if it consumes you. It confounds me that you and others like you are the most interesting people around. As I've said to you before, your life is illogical; it has no balance or variety. There is no restraint. Common sense is absent. Most of the rest of us never find such things to do, or else we have the good sense to resist them if we do. We can never lay ourselves open to such trials…such outlandish sacrifices. To us, you and your kind are merely victims of obsessions you cannot control."

The stranger paused to stare at the artist, who continued working and gave no sign that he was even listening.

"Still, when you succeed," continued the stranger, "you sometimes produce things that positively fascinate us. We flock to them. We debate and argue over them. We acclaim them. In the end, we prize them. We may even eventually claim these productions as our own: our French art."

The stranger knew by now that he was talking to himself. The demeanor of Cézanne, his bodily movement and concentration on his work, made it perfectly clear that his words were not in the least impressing themselves on the mind of the artist, who was by now utterly lost in his own world of thought and action. But as if it didn't matter, the stranger just went on talking out loud, now more to himself than to his obstinate audience. Even though he knew that Cézanne was no longer listening, the stranger could not stop his words from taking on an accusatory tone. "You've hardly even traveled, have you? Except for your infernal back-and-forths between Paris and Aix. Once to Switzerland, dragged there against your will by your wife. You call yourself an artist, and you haven't even been to Italy, although you live almost on its borders. Do you know that Florence is closer to Aix than Paris? And Rome is not much farther. For more than 200 years, French artists have dreamed of going to Rome to see and study the great patrimony of ancient Rome and the Renaissance…but not you."

Continuing to stare at the painter, the stranger waved his hand in a gesture of disdain. "You have nothing to say, do you? Well, there's no need. I know the answer. For you, your Louvre is enough art. And for the rest, it's your beloved rocks and trees and all those silly apples and jars. Nature itself, you'd say. That's all you need, and I suppose you're right. Look at you there.

You're like a member of one of those arcane orders of monks who spend all their waking hours praying for humanity, praying daily for the salvation of the world while the rest of us go on our merry ways. Except instead of praying for us, you have appointed yourself to do our seeing. You sit for hours daily, staring at the world, probing its secrets in order to...in order to...who knows what? To show it to us, I suppose. To teach us what is there. And of course we pay no more attention to you than to them."

"Than to whom?" asked Cézanne, suddenly rousing himself from his work.

"Than the monks who pray for us, dammit! You aren't listening to me, are you?"

The artist seemed confused. Then he shrugged and turned back again to his work.

"What's the use? Look at him...staring at his painting with the loyalty and patience of an old dog. As if the whole world were there. He doesn't even know I'm here anymore. Well, why not? That's what he's about. That's all he's ever been about. And nobody is going to change him.

"So what am I bothering for? Why am I wasting my time? It's been the same with all the others I've tracked down. What infernal thing makes me do this? For reasons I do not understand, I am compelled to seek out these obsessed people and follow them around, trying to talk them out of their obsessions! Of course, I never can. That certain people can give their lives so totally and single-mindedly to one unique pursuit drives me crazy. They've found some meaning to their lives that eludes me. Well, I can't tolerate that. Of course, I can't stop it either. It's the nature and depth of the commitment that I can't stand, especially in the ones who never seem to get anywhere. They just go on and on, and I don't know why."

The stranger looked at the hillside the artist was studying. He tried to see what in particular attracted Cézanne to this site but could not see what it was. To him it just seemed like an indifferent view of some trees and a hill. He sighed.

"Well, what's the use? There's nothing left here; we've had our little say. You're right, I should go away and leave you in peace."

Struck by a sudden thought, the stranger reached into a pocket of his coat and withdrew a watchcase. He opened it, noted the time, and spoke quietly to himself. "If I leave now, I can catch the tram to Marseilles and then the night train to Paris. The billiards championship between Vigneau and that American challenger, Sutton, begins tomorrow. Besides, I must be in Paris in order to wait for that young Italian—what's his name?—something Modigliani. He has great promise to be an especially interesting case. Utterly obsessed by painting, a hopeless failure, and maybe more. Delicious!"

The decision made, the stranger moved purposefully. He picked up his satchel, looked around one last time, and in a final pass at the artist said, "It's going to rain tomorrow. Don't get caught out in it."

The old painter did not answer; he did not even hear the stranger's words. Bent over his canvas, he was lost in thought, analyzing his sensations, dreaming his dreams.

13

House Below a Ridge
(A Painting in Progress)

/light/

/falling to the left/

SKY

Blue toward redd...ish......mauve

   cobalt...blue (lightened)

       The still white plane...

reflects the (light) blue light of the cobalt sky

         (toward green) (toward red)

Strokes of blue-green sky, aslant

   rise through the plane...   sky plane

     blue   bluer... paler

RIDGE

Planes intersect...ridge&sky   The blue plane-sky

   descends upon the brown-green ridge (where exactly?) (how exactly?)

Ridgedge...rich edge...richer...   redder (turning back to blue)

     Siennas...ochers...umbers...(raw) (yellow) (burnt)

The bare, red-orange earth...blue tinted (air)

   skirts the blue-green trees (red tinted, yellow tinted).

(The top of one blue-green tree forsakes the safety of the ridge

   to probe the infinite blue plane.)

TREES

Trunks dividing space   (enclosing, isolating)

  Branches crossing...arching...green reaching to blue...reaching to
chrome yellow...reach...ing to...*laque de garance.*

Foliages outspread...

  many colored leaves toward blue...toward yellow...toward red...
    enfolding many greens.

Horizons (never stable) shift...disappear...reappear...

  redefining themselves (& each other)...with every move of eye...

                                    every turn of head.

HOUSE

(red-roofed, yellow walled, blue doored, gabled)

Pale yellow walls (rose and many whites)

  set against viridian trees.

TREES (again)

Greens (as above)   red tinted...yellow tinted...

    lighter...lighter...

  touched by red...by Prussian blue...by white...

      more white...more...

AFTERWORD: Witness

PLEASE DON'T CLOSE THE BOOK YET. I know the author here has told you the story he wants to tell, and I'm all right with that. After all, why not? There are already so many theories and ideas out there about Paul and his art that there might as well be another, and you, dear reader, will have to make up your own mind about them just the same. The fact is that the life of my friend Paul Cézanne is so complicated and rich in events, anecdotes, and mystery that anyone who writes about him seems to create another Cézanne.

As for me, I can tell you that while I know a lot about Paul, I certainly don't want to write another book about him. God knows how many more will be written without my adding another to the shelves. And just now you've read one more! I've only come forward now to confirm a thing or two, maybe elaborate a little bit here and there, and fill in one or two gaps.

But before I do that, I suppose I ought to introduce myself. As you can see, I'm not Paul, and I'm certainly not that voice you heard throughout the book, the author, who seems to know so much. No, I'm not either of them, but my name probably doesn't mean anything to you. It was mentioned just once in the book. The only way you might know who I am would be if you read other books about Paul Cézanne.

My name is Solari. Philippe Solari. I'm a sculptor. At least I was while I was still alive. I made it to the Salon a few times, too. Yes, I had my work seen right there in the Palais de l'Industrie like all the others who survived those insufferable juries. But I've no illusions about all that anymore. That was a long time ago. I know that if I have any claim to fame now, it's because I knew him. Paul Cézanne was a fellow artist, and he was my friend. We're both from the same town, in fact, Aix-en-Provence.

Oh, I know what some of you are probably thinking, but I did enjoy a tiny reputation as an artist in my day, not in Paris, of course, but in Aix. After all, when I was gone, they named a street after me. That was nice, but let's face it, compared to Paul, I'm small potatoes.

As far as remembrance goes, there are quite a few of us from Aix whose memory is dependent upon our associations with him. Besides me, there's Achille Emperaire, Numa Coste, Joseph Villevieille, Antony Valabrègue, Marius Roux, and a good many others whose names you've not heard of either and who weren't mentioned in this book. As I just said, likely the only place you'll ever hear about us now is in biographies about Paul, and, oh my, are there a lot of those!

Or else maybe—come to think of it—you might hear of us in a book or two about Émile Zola, who didn't really appear in this book but who was talked about more than once. He was part of our little circle too, although he wasn't born in Aix. I'm not sure the author made that as clear as he might have. Émile came along a little later when we were all in school.

But who could have guessed? Right there in our midst, such a painter!

He stood out among us even back at the beginning, though at first more for his temperament than for his art. The author made this point, but I want you to hear it from me, from somebody who knew him. God, he was difficult! I'm not exaggerating.

You never knew what he would do from one minute to the

next. One day he'd be as friendly as could be. Easy. High-spirited.
And the next day, just to avoid you, he'd cross the street if he saw
you coming. These mood swings, which didn't get any better as
the years went by, were a burden to his friends but most of all to
himself.

Even in old Gibert's drawing class at the museum—that was
back in '58 or so, when we did all those old classical drawings
after sculptures and models—it was bad. None of us was exempt
from his wrath. The slightest word could send him off. You never
knew why. You never knew what you'd said or done. He'd just
throw up his arms and storm off. Even the slightest encounter
with someone unknown could be a disaster.

I know I'm reminiscing here, and I hope you will pardon me.
The author has already given you a pretty good idea of Paul's
unpredictable nature, but it's still fascinating to think about. I
never knew anyone else quite like him.

Here's a little incident the author doesn't know, but which
I personally witnessed. Listen to this. It's so typical. I was with
him once in the woods around Aix. This was in the later years.
We were both working separately, a good distance apart. Paul
was painting, of course, when this man came along. Neither one
of us had ever seen him before. In the most innocent way, this
person went up to Paul's easel and glanced at the painting that
was there. Then he smiled and nodded to Paul and went on his
way. Not a word was spoken either way. Now I ask you, what
was the harm in that? But as soon as the man was gone, Paul was
furious. He was so upset he couldn't continue working. Why?
Who knows? Maybe he thought there was a tinge of contempt
or ridicule in the man's smile. Maybe he thought that this man
had intruded into his personal space in some rude way. I don't
know, but that's just how touchy he could be. That was true to

form, you might say.

Another time I was out walking with him in the woods, when he pointed out to me a site he said he would love to paint. He discussed it with me in the greatest detail, patiently showing me how just about every rock and tree limb played a part in what he called his motif. You read about these motifs. Maybe you've made some sense of them. I never could. He was always talking about motifs.

He must have spent hours analyzing that patch of ground. I never knew anything like it. He had never talked to me like that before. He was obviously moved by what he saw there, and by the time he was finished telling me about it, I was very excited to see him start this new work. But when I said this to him, he lowered his head and fell silent. When I persisted, he said, "No, I'm not going to do this painting. I don't like it here. People will come by and see me working." Honestly, I'm not exaggerating. Isn't that odd? Why should he give up a beautiful site to paint only because someone might walk by and look at what he was doing? Notice that I said *might*. The piece of ground we were looking at wasn't very close to any paths or trails, and the chance of somebody walking by wasn't great. But that's how he was.

All his friends could tell similar stories. All of us were the observers or the victims of his strange behavior. And you don't need to believe just me. You heard Monet, Renoir, and Pissarro tell even stranger tales about him. Isn't it odd sometimes to see the kinds of people in whom great talent comes to roost? All that genius dwelling in such a peculiar, jumpy, unstable fellow.

Anyway, I can certainly vouch for those parts of the book here that tell about the way Paul worked at his painting. We all knew the troubles he had when he was doing his work. There was no one else like him. All that time he took and all those anxieties and doubts he experienced are accurate. Your author there was right about that. Just as he says, Paul could spend hours laboring over exactly where to put everything in a still life or worrying over every twig and rock in a landscape. It was something to see, if he ever let you watch, which he almost never did. The author got that right too.

Those other parts, though, where the author goes on and on about seeing? I don't know about that. You'll just have to make up your own mind. To me, seeing is seeing, and that's all there is to it. Why make such a fuss?

But I haven't come here to talk about how Paul made his art. That's too complicated. At least it is for me. Besides, you know now that he mostly did his painting in such secrecy. Only rarely would he let any of us near him while he worked, which, if you don't mind my saying, does kind of make you wonder how the author here thinks he knows so much in such detail. In my recollection, none of us really knew what he was doing most of the time. He sort of lived like a hermit, working away there, unwatched. He might as well have been living high up on a mountain in a cave somewhere.

But we were always interested in him. After all—and I'm sure you agree—he was such a character. His personality went back and forth between such extremes. And that's mostly what I can tell you about. How such a high-strung, nervous, even frightened man could paint the way he did amazed even us. And we knew him better than most, I guess. But even after all these years, it's still hard to believe. Why, even Pissarro said Paul was unbalanced.

Don't misunderstand me. If I say he was my friend, I don't mean that I was one of his intimates, at least not until the later years. I was never like Zola, for instance; nobody was ever as close to Paul as he was. The author in his story here has that stranger fellow mention the relationship between Paul and Émile, and as far as he went, he got that right. But in my opinion, a lot more could be said about that. Émile was really very special for a long time in Paul's life.

I don't want to go into all the stuff about Paul and Émile in their early days when they were schoolboys, but that's how far back their friendship went. It's enough to say that they built a deep friendship from the beginning and that Émile was a very generous and sturdy friend of Paul's for decades. That is, until '86, when he wrote that book, *The Masterpiece*, about Paul and all his artist friends. You read a little about it there in Chapter 3. You heard Paul and the stranger going back and forth about that. Something happened then that still is not really clear. Oh, there was a break—no doubt about that—but the reasons are complicated. Surely Émile's book figured into it. As you know, Paul never wrote or spoke to Émile again. That was too bad.

But, you know, there were parts of that book I enjoyed, and so did the others. Émile may have shown his true colors to us about art—and how little he actually understood it or us—but he also wrote wonderfully about many good times we all had. He gave us all fictitious names, as you know. Paul was Lantier, of course, and Émile called himself Sandoz. And just think, he named me Mahoudeau. And not only that, but he wrote in great detail about the hilarious time my sculpture collapsed just before I had to submit it to the Salon jury. I wasn't laughing at the time. Paul was there when it happened, and so were Manet and Émile. I was so poor in those days I didn't even have enough money to build a proper armature to support this large, pretty heavy nude I was building in plaster. It was the dead of winter, and after I got a fire going in my studio, the heat made the old bits of chairs and broomsticks crack and the piece collapsed. You should have seen it. But even after that, we managed to salvage enough of it to submit it. Under another title, of course.

Such a pity about that book. As bad an impact as Émile's book had on us all, there were some really great times recorded there.

Come to think of it, '86 was a big year for Paul. Besides his break with Émile, he married Hortense, who had given him a son fourteen years before, and late in the year his father died. This last event made Paul a rich man. His father, of course, was that banker the author mentioned. But while old Mr. Cézanne lived, he kept Paul on a very short string. He never approved of Paul's choice of career. As you've already read, he always wanted to see Paul do something "respectable," such as banking or the law. Can you imagine Paul Cézanne as a lawyer? Ha! All those glorious paintings of his could have been legal mumbo-jumbo. Think of it. Contracts, deeds, and wills instead of portraits, landscapes, and still lifes. Ridiculous! But you heard Paul and the stranger argue about all that, and, boy, did they go after each other, right? I think Paul may have hated the stranger almost as much as he hated Gauguin.

And then if you couple that with his obsession with Frenhofer, you start to get a strange picture. Poor Paul was driven by his own special set of demons. In fact, the author's imaginative leap to the stranger coming upon Paul at work is not such a great one, if you think about Frenhofer. Paul had an imagination both fearful and spectacular. His fears and doubts could drive him to mysterious, even outlandish places in his mind, while his artistic genius and tenacity raised him to sublime artistic heights. That's what makes Paul Cézanne so fascinating.

I heard somebody recently use the word "paranoid" to

describe Paul. I never heard anyone use that word back in the old days, but maybe it's a good word here. Maybe Paul was touched by a little bit of paranoia. Anyway, that's more than I know about. I'm just telling you what I hear these days.

Well, as I said before, although I knew him almost my whole life, I was never really intimate with Paul until the later years. I'd see him here and there. In Paris. In Aix. Once we even lived in the same building in Paris on the Rue de Chevreuse. That was just for four or five months back in '72.

But when I wasn't directly in touch with Paul, I'd hear about him from others. Paul was always worth some gossip. Our little circle was always interested in what he was doing, what he was painting. There was always a rumor, a whisper. What would he send this year to the Salon? How would he insult the jurors this time? How would he shock them?

I remember once when a group of us paraded his huge canvas through the streets of Paris in a wheelbarrow on the last day of submissions. This was the period when Paul made a lot of those outrageous paintings, the dark and violent ones that set the juries in an uproar. Back in the '60s, say. But what a stir we made that day! What fun we had! On days like that you'd think Paul had thrown off all his hesitations, all his doubts. He seemed almost reckless in the way he tried to take the Salon by storm. But you know what I think? This was just another way to hide. He always sent a painting he knew would be rejected. Among us, he wore his rejections like medals, and we were all proud of him. Underneath it all, though, I think he was hurting. Rejections of any kind always preyed on his mind. He paid a price for his bravado.

Then in the '70s he worked outdoors in the countryside with Pissarro for a while. This was hugely important, as your author there has noted. He changed his approach to things then in a big way. Fewer and fewer of those strange, dark paintings. This began the period when he started to paint in the way we all like to think of him now: the landscapes, the still lifes, the portraits, and so forth. That time with Pissarro marks where he really began to find himself as an artist. You might say that was the time when his brain took control of his emotions and he started down a long and sometimes painful path toward some new way of seeing and thinking about painting. Some say it was profound what he did when he was with Pissarro. Pissarro got him outdoors looking at the real world, that's for sure. That was when it all really started.

So there are some of the extremes about my friend. They are odd enough, no doubt, but for all that, there's the other part. By that I mean, the Paul Cézanne who overcame all these difficulties both within himself and from outside himself and who left us a body of work that, if I understand the acclaim today, is loved and admired around the world. How do you explain it? Such a man—so unstable, so extreme—who nevertheless is thought by many to be one of the greatest painters France has ever produced.

These later years were the period when Paul and I were the closest. I was there in Aix; we'd known each other, you might say, all our adult lives. We were both getting on in years then. We were comfortable together. Like two old dogs, we were. Anyway, most of his other friends were not around. Some of them were dead. That's how we came together, I suppose. It was a kind of convenience at first, but I flatter myself that in the end the feelings between us were genuine and deep.

Oh, we had some good times, the two of us. I'd have dinner at his place, or he at mine. Madame Cézanne was a marvelous cook. Of course, I'm talking about Paul's mother and not his wife Hortense, the other Madame Cézanne. She was kind of a pill, if you ask me. Besides, she was almost always off somewhere. Paris or Switzerland. At some spa or other, usually with their son in tow. She hated Aix, and I can't say as I blame her. Nobody there was really nice to her. They always treated her like an outsider. She spent a lot of Paul's money. She used to drive him crazy with her trips and her extravagances.

Later on when Paul's son grew up, Paul turned more and more to him for help through the difficulties of life. And it was the women, too—his mother and sisters—who got him back into the church. He used to laugh it off, calling it a kind of insurance policy for a man getting on in years, but he'd go regularly to church on Sundays unless, of course, he got angry at the priest, which he did from time to time.

Paul's mother died in 1897, and after Paul and his two sisters sold the Jas, I'd dine with him sometimes at his place in town, or else maybe we'd go together either to my place or perhaps to Rosa Berne's little auberge in Le Tholonet. Paul was especially fond of Rosa's duck with olives.

And in those days we'd work together too. We'd go off to the rock quarry, him to paint, me to work on one of my sculpture projects. He sat for me from time to time. I did two busts of him, one from memory. He didn't like either of them much. He never said so outright, but I could tell. That's all right.

Sometimes we'd talk late into the night. Occasionally, if we drank a little too much wine, we'd get into rousing arguments about art. Our shouting brought the neighbors out of their houses more than once. He could talk your head off, you know. Most people didn't realize that. People always thought he was so gruff and withdrawn. But if he felt really comfortable with the folks he was with and his mood was just right, then he could spout opinions and theories about art and artists all night long. He'd talk about Manet, Pissarro, and Monet. He loved Delacroix, Poussin, Rubens, the Le Nain brothers. I couldn't always follow what he was saying, but that didn't matter. I never had much of a head for theories; I just made my sculpture when I could.

I should also say we had other times together when hardly a word passed between us. He could go into what seemed like a trance in front of one of his still lifes on a table there in his studio. He'd stare at those bottles and apples as if they were the whole world. Personally, I could never really understand what he was looking at. They were just plain old bottles and apples, nothing special, as far I could see. What was he thinking about? I never could figure it out.

There's more I could say, but I think I've told you enough. I just want you to understand that I was there too. I was part of Paul's life, and all his friends and colleagues were also colleagues and friends of mine. I was there with them, and I watched them all go through the good times and the bad. All the ups and downs, the trials, the scorn, the rejections, and eventually the successes. I saw it all. Paul had to take the hardest road, not that he didn't bring a lot of his troubles down on himself. As you've already gathered, Paul was such a complicated person. He was his own worst enemy.

I personally think too many books and articles have been written about my friend Paul, but that's only my opinion. I have to admit that the art and life of my friend seem to inspire more and more books and articles, not to mention exhibitions, reproductions, and such. It's been an endless flood since Paul died. But as you have probably noticed, I'm not an intellectual. To me art is just art.

On the other hand, I've heard lately that there are some well-known writers on art who say there's nothing more to be said about Paul and his art. Meaningful writing about Paul's art is finished, they say. Done. One of them even said he was now bored by it. Well, if writing about Paul Cézanne from now on is a waste of time, that's a big surprise. Personally, I don't think it's Paul and his art that's exhausted, but the writers themselves. Poor fellows.

Well, I'll be on my way now. Thanks for letting me have my say. Farewell.

ABOUT THE AUTHOR

WALTER E. THOMPSON was born in San Francisco, California. He graduated from San Francisco State College with a B.A., and later from the University of Michigan with a Ph.D. in art history. He taught art and art history in several liberal arts institutions in Illinois and South Carolina. He has been a practicing painter throughout his adult life. Since 1983 he has lived in New York. Most recently he and his wife reside in a small, rural community in Columbia County, north of the city.